EXCITING TIMES

EXCITING TIMES

A NOVEL

NAOISE DOLAN

ecco
An Imprint of HarperCollins*Publishers*

HarperCollins books may be purchased for educational, business, or sales promotional use. For information, please email the Special Markets Department at SPsales@harpercollins.com.

Ecco® and HarperCollins® are trademarks of HarperCollins Publishers.

FIRST EDITION

Designed by Michelle Crowe

Library of Congress Cataloging-in-Publication Data

Names: Dolan, Naoise, 1992– author.
Title: Exciting times : a novel / Naoise Dolan.
Description: New York : Ecco, [2020] |
Identifiers: LCCN 2019050717 (print) | LCCN 2019050718 (ebook) | ISBN 9780062968746 (hardcover) | ISBN 9780062968753 (trade paperback) | ISBN 9780062968777 (ebook)
Classification: LCC PR6104.O49 E93 2020 (print) | LCC PR6104.O49 (ebook) | DDC 823/.92—dc23
LC record available at https://lccn.loc.gov/2019050717
LC ebook record available at https://lccn.loc.gov/

20 21 22 23 24   LSC   10 9 8 7 6 5 4 3

For my grandmother

PART I

JULIAN

JULY 2016

My banker friend Julian first took me for lunch in July, the month I arrived in Hong Kong. I'd forgotten which exit of the station we were meeting at, but he called saying he saw me outside Kee Wah Bakery and to wait there. It was humid. Briefcase-bearers clopped out of turnstiles like breeding jennets. The Tannoy blared out first Cantonese, then Mandarin, and finally a British woman saying please mind the gap.

Through the concourse and up the escalators, we talked about how crowded Hong Kong was. Julian said London was calmer, and I said Dublin was, too. At the restaurant he put his phone facedown on the table, so I did the same, as if for me, too, this represented a professional sacrifice. Mindful he'd be paying, I asked if he'd like water—but while I was asking, he took the jug and poured.

"Work's busy," he said. "I barely know what the hell I'm doing."

Bankers often said that. The less knowledge they professed, the more they knew and the higher their salary.

I asked where he'd lived before Hong Kong, and he said he'd read history at Oxford. People who'd gone to Oxford would tell you so even when it wasn't the question. Then, like "everyone," he'd gone to the City. "Which city?" I said. Julian assessed whether women made jokes, decided we did, and laughed. I said I didn't know where I'd end up. He asked how old I was, I said I'd just turned twenty-two, and he told me I was a baby and I'd figure it out.

We ate our salads and he asked if I'd dated in Hong Kong yet. I said not really, feeling "yet" did contradictory things as an adverb and there were more judicious choices he could have made. In Ireland, I said, you didn't "date." You hooked up, and after a while you came to an understanding.

Julian said: "So you're saying it's like London."

"I don't know," I said. "I've never been."

"You've 'never been' to London."

"No."

"Ever?"

"Never," I said, pausing long enough to satisfy him that I'd tried to change this fact about my personal history upon his second query and was very sorry I'd failed.

"Ava," he said, "that's incredible."

"Why?"

"It's such a short flight from Dublin."

I was disappointed in me, too. He'd never been to Ireland, but it would have been redundant to tell him it was also a short flight that way.

We discussed headlines. He'd read in the *FT* that the offshore renminbi was down against the dollar. The one piece of news I could offer was that a tropical storm was coming. "Yes," he said, "Mirinae. And a typhoon the week after." We agreed it was an exciting time to be alive.

Both storms came. Unrelatedly, we kept getting lunch. "I'm glad we're friends," he'd say, and far be it from me to correct a Balliol man. I felt spending time with him would make me smarter, or would at least prepare me to talk about currencies and indices with the serious people I would encounter in the course of adult life. We got on well. I enjoyed his money and he enjoyed how easily impressed I was by it.

I 'd been sad in Dublin, decided it was Dublin's fault, and thought
Hong Kong would help.

My TEFL school was in a pastel-towered commercial dis-
trict. They only hired white people but made sure not to put that in
writing. Like sharks' teeth, teachers dropped out and were replaced.
Most were backpackers who left once they'd saved enough to find
themselves in Thailand. I had no idea who I was, but doubted the
Thais would know either. Because I lacked warmth, I was mainly assigned grammar classes, where children not liking you was a positive
performance indicator. I found this an invigorating respite from how
people usually assessed women.

Students came for weekly lessons. We taught back to back, besides
lunch. I became known as the resident Lady Muck for stealing away
between lessons to urinate.

"Ava, where were you?" said Joan, my manager—one, holy, and ap-
ostolic, which there was money in being, though not Catholic since
there wasn't—when I returned from a toilet break. She was one of the
first Hongkongers I'd met.

"It was five minutes," I said.

"Where are the minutes coming from?" said Joan. "Parents pay for sixty per week."

"What if I end the class slightly early?" I said. "Then start the next one slightly late. Two minutes from one, two from the other."

"But that's two from the start and two from the end of the middle class." Joan tried to gesticulate, but found it difficult to mime a three-class sandwich as a two-hand person. She abandoned the endeavor with a tart sigh like this was my fault.

I needed to take it to a higher power.

Our director, Benny, was forty and wore a baseball cap backwards, either to look like he loved working with kids or to stress that he was his own boss and dressed to please no one, not even himself. Hong Kong–born, Canadian-educated, repatriated, and thriving, he owned a dozen other schools and—evocatively, I felt—an Irish seaweed company. He spoke of this last as "back" in Connemara, a place neither of us had been, though I supposed that enhanced the poetry of it. The buck stopped with him, a reflection of his general distaste for parting with currency.

When Benny came at the end of July to pay me, I said I was thinking of leaving.

"Why?" he said. "You've been here a month."

"I need to go to the toilet between classes. I'll get a UTI if I don't."

"You're not quitting over that."

He was right. Aside from anything else, I hadn't quit over their racist recruitment policy, so it would have been weird to leave just because I couldn't piss whenever I wanted.

I knew I'd do anything for money. Throughout college back in Ireland, I'd kept a savings account that I charmingly termed "abortion fund." It had €1,500 in it by the end. I knew some women who saved with their friends, and they all helped whoever was unlucky. But I didn't trust anyone. I got the money together by waitressing, then kept adding to it after I had enough for a procedure in England. I liked watching the balance go up. The richer I got, the harder it would be for anyone to force me to do anything.

Just before leaving for Hong Kong, I sat my final exams. While they were handing out the papers, I counted how many hours I'd waited tables. Weeks of my life were in that savings account. For as long as I lived in Ireland, and for as long as abortion was illegal there, I'd have to keep my dead time locked up.

That evening I used most of the money to book a flight to Hong Kong and a room for the first month, and started applying for teaching jobs. I left Dublin three weeks later.

The week I started, they told me the common features of Hong Kong English and said to correct the children when they used them. "I go already" to mean "I went," that was wrong, though I understood it fine after the first few days. "Lah" for emphasis—no lah, sorry lah—wasn't English. I saw no difference between that and Irish people putting "sure" in random places, it served a similar function sure, but that wasn't English either. English was British.

AUGUST

Julian wasn't bothered coming out to meet me after work, so I started going straight to his apartment in Mid-Levels at about 9 p.m. I told him I found this awkward and degrading. Actually I liked taking the outdoor escalator up. I got on the covered walkway at Queen's Road and went uphill over hawker stalls on Stanley Street, then signs—Game & Fun, Happy Massage, King Tailor—and high-rises and enormous windows on Wellington Street. Then came fishy air wafting up from Central Street Market and the old police station stacked with thick white bricks like pencil erasers. When I reached Julian's building, I got a visitor card from the lobby and went up to the fiftieth floor.

Inside, his apartment looked like a showroom, the sort that had been unconvincingly scattered with items anyone could have owned. His most obviously personal possession was a large gray MacBook Pro.

We got takeaway, I did the washing up, and then he'd pour us wine and we'd talk in the sitting room. The mantelpiece was bare besides an empty silver picture frame and cream candles that had never been lit. By the window was a long brown corner sofa. I'd take my shoes off and lie on it with my feet on the armrest, crossing one leg over the other and alternating them during gaps in the conversation.

He smoked cheap cigarettes—to encourage himself to quit, he said.

We'd first met in the smoking area of a bar in Lan Kwai Fong, where he'd either noticed me looking at him, or started looking at me first until I looked back. He was good at engineering ambiguities. I was bad at avoiding them. He'd said everything very slowly that night, so I'd assumed he was drunk—but he still did it sober, so I gathered he was rich.

A month into our acquaintance, he asked: "Do you meet all your friends in bars?"

"I don't have any friends," I said. He laughed.

In some moods he told me about markets. In others he'd fire questions at me, only attending to my answers to the extent that they helped him think of follow-up inquiries. I'd said it before, but he wanted to hear it all again—the two brothers, the brown terraced house in one of Dublin's drearier suburbs, that I'd taken a year out after school to save up for college. That after 2008 I shared a room with my brother Tom so we could rent the other one out to a student. That none of this made us poor and was in fact pretty much what had happened to Ireland as a whole, due in no small part to the actions of banks like his.

Julian had gone to Eton and was an only child. These were the two least surprising facts anyone had ever told me about themselves.

He wanted to know if my accent was posh where I came from. I'd never met an English person who didn't wonder that. Most wouldn't ask outright—and he didn't, he just asked what "kind" of Dublin accent I had—but they found some way to convey their curiosity. I told him it was a normal Dublin accent. He asked what that meant. I didn't know enough about British accents to make a comparison.

"Well," he said, "how does a posh Dublin accent sound?"

I tried to do one and he said it sounded American.

He'd ask what I proposed to do with myself when the time came to get a real job. He was almost paternally adamant that I shouldn't waste my degree on lowly employers, and even paid convincing lip service to not thinking less of me for not having gone to Oxford. But when it came to which jobs he did consider good enough for me, he was vague. Law was glorified clerking. Consulting was flying to the middle of nowhere to piss around with PowerPoint. Accountancy was boring and didn't pay well. And banking, in some nebulous way, wouldn't suit me.

I liked when he rolled up his shirtsleeves. He had big square wrists and jutting elbows. Sometimes I worried he could tell how often I thought about his arms. He was always calling me a freak for other, much less strange things, so I couldn't own up to it.

The first time I stayed in the guest room was in mid-August when the tropical storm Dianmu hit. After that, Julian always offered to put me up when midnight approached. Depending on my energy, I accepted or got the green minibus home—the covered escalator only went one direction at a time: down for morning rush hour or up for the rest of the day.

That was the shape of it, but it didn't have a name, apart from hanging out, catching up, or popping in for a chat, which was, to be fair, the content of what we were doing. He was so stretched for time that I found it semi-plausible he just preferred to meet in his apartment for convenience.

I asked whether bankers had time for relationships.

"Usually not at the junior levels," he said. "A lot of them just pay for it."

The way he said "it" made me uneasy, but there wasn't any point in taking things up with Banker Julian. He was too self-assured to notice when I criticized him. He registered that I'd said something, then continued a parallel conversation.

When he paid for my takeaway, or when he took me to a restaurant, and when in return I spent time with him, I wondered if he saw himself as paying for a milder "it." I liked the idea—my company being worth money. No one else accorded it that value. We sat in high-ceilinged rooms and he said the Hang Seng was down and the

Shenzhen Composite was up and the Shanghai Composite was flat. It wasn't like normal friendships where I worried if the other person still liked me. He liked hearing himself think aloud and I reasoned that I was profiting from it, that you never knew when you'd need facts so it was best to collect as many as you could.

One night in his living room, a few glasses into the bottle, I told him he was attractive. I said it exactly like that—"I find you attractive"—to avoid seeming earnest.

"You're quite attractive, too," he said.

"I guess that's why we get along."

"Could be."

We'd known each other about two months, and in total I'd spent perhaps thirty hours in his company—little more than a day. But I was in the habit of thinking he was a habit.

"Thanks for your time," he'd say as I left. I wasn't sure if he put it formally to give himself an ironic get-out clause like I did, or if he was just unaware how stiff he sounded. He'd add: "I'll text you." He seemed to think only a man could initiate a conversation. Worse still, it meant I couldn't send him one first. It would look like I'd despaired of his getting in contact and was only doing it myself as a last resort.

I explained to my nine-year-olds that there were two ways to say the "th" sound. The one at the start of "think" and the end of "tooth" was the voiceless dental fricative, and the one at the start of "that," "these," and "those" was the voiced dental fricative. As a Dubliner, I had gone twenty-two years without knowingly pronouncing either phoneme. If anyone had thought there was something wrong with my English, they'd kept it to themselves. Now I had to practice fricatives, voiced and un-, so the kids could copy me.

Calvin Jong—a show-off, but a useful one—volunteered to try, and couldn't do it.

"Hold your tongue still and breathe," I said. That was what the teacher's guide told me to say, but I tried it myself and produced a sound unlike anything I had ever heard from an English speaker, or indeed from any other vertebrate in the animal kingdom. I decided I'd ask Julian to show me how to do it later.

———

Even before I met Julian, I didn't often see my flatmates. We exchanged little more than hellos and goodnights.

There were three of us. I'd booked the room on Airbnb, planning to be there until I could save up a deposit for something more permanent, but the others lived there long-term. Emily was the oldest and the most proactive. At twenty-nine, she'd been in Hong Kong a few years. Freya was around my age and her chief hobby was complaining about her job. She changed into her pajamas the minute she got in the door and had four sets of house slippers: bedroom, bathroom, kitchen, other.

Emily always had comments when I came in. "Could you close the fridge more quietly?" was this particular evening's criticism.

"Sorry," I said. I failed to see how you could make noise shutting a refrigerator, but Emily had an aesthetic sensibility.

Them getting ready woke me up—spoons clanging on bowls, taps protesting on being asked to produce water—but I couldn't brush my teeth until the bathroom was free. I lay there and ran my tongue over the night's accumulated plaque. We often got cockroaches. I swore I heard Emily and Freya in the dark, though I knew scientifically this couldn't be true. I went without eating rather than face talking to them in the kitchen. They weren't that bad. I just never knew what to say to them.

So staying over with Julian became ever more appealing.

4

SEPTEMBER

After about two months, I was spending a few nights a week at his flat. The spare room—mine now, I supposed—had a soft twill houndstooth throw and pictures of London on the wall. One day at work I printed out an image of Dublin and asked if I could put it in the empty frame in the living room. "If you like," he said. He told me I was welcome to stay over while he was traveling for work, but I didn't. The temptation to go poking around his bedroom would have been overwhelming. The inside was still a mystery to me, but I imagined everything folded and stored in optimized locations for speedy access.

One evening when he was abroad, I came home to the Airbnb and Emily ambushed me before I could get to my room.

"We haven't seen much of you lately," she said.

"We can't all be here at once," I said. "It's claustrophobic."

"Let's go for drinks, then."

"Sure," I said. "When?"

"Tomorrow?"

Julian was back from Singapore then. "Sorry," I said. "I'm having dinner with a friend."

"Is this the friend you stay over with?"

"I don't have that many friends."

Emily began to tidy the ugly couch cushions, as if hoping I'd notice how good she was for not asking me to help. The fabric had a talent for gathering hairs: hers and Freya's mostly, since I was never there, but they blamed me anyway.

"You can't drop everything for a guy," she said.

"I'm not with him."

"Why are you always at his place?"

I'd stopped listening. If she wanted to complain about me never being there, but offer extensive notes whenever I did make an appearance, then no wonder I preferred Julian.

———

The next evening, I narrated the argument to Julian. Between drags of his cigarette, he nodded and of-coursed in all the right places.

"Have you ever had flatmates?" I said.

"Yes, of course, at Oxford, and when I was starting out in London. Most of them were fine. One guy was a complete nutter. This was my final year of uni. He was doing his dissertation on some existential quandary. You'd hear him pacing around all night muttering about it. And he never ate solid food—he put everything in this big fucking blender. Lived on smoothies. I think he got the top first in his year."

"So having your own place is better?"

"Substantially better."

Neither of us pointed out that he didn't really live alone anymore. We finished the wine and he went to get another bottle. My jeans had a hole on the inseam near the top of my thigh. I picked at it, then jerked my hand away when I heard him returning.

I said: "What was your last girlfriend like?"

He twirled his glass. "She was fine. She got sent back to London."

"How long ago was that?"

"A few months."

"Any regrets?"

"No, none at all. I don't tend to look back."

We drank our wine and enjoyed each other's silence. His cushions, I noticed, were beautiful: pebble corduroy, gold and ivory sateen. I picked one up and hugged it to my chest.

"That thing you said before about wanting to be a history teacher," I said, "were you really just bullshitting me?"

"Completely. I'm glad other people do it, but for my part I'd rather hang on to the dim prospect of owning a house."

He'd said that thing about teaching history the first time we met, and I hadn't been sure if he was joking. I still wasn't. I said: "What if you could own a house no matter what you did?"

"I've never thought about that because it's certainly not happening in our lifetimes. Possibly I'd have stayed at Oxford and done more history. But there's no point dwelling on it. I have every respect for people who follow their passions, but I prefer stability."

I wondered if he meant his comment to have point.

"It could be worse," I said. "You could have no passions and also no stability."

"To be clear, Ava: we're both dead behind the eyes, but at least I can pay rent?"

"Pretty much."

"We really are the new belle époque."

"Arsehole bankers and deadbeats."

"Not all bankers are arseholes."

"Yeah, just you."

"Just me."

"I like talking to you," I said—quite stupidly, I realized. "It makes me feel solid, like someone can confirm I'm real."

"Good."

"Do you like having me here?"

"Yes," he said. "You're good company. And if I've got this space and I like sharing it with you, there's no reason not to."

"You mean it suits you."

"Not 'suits.' You're making me sound calculating. I'm saying it makes sense."

He seemed closer to me on the couch than he had a moment ago, although he hadn't moved.

"If it stopped making sense, would you stop asking me over?" I said.

"You mean would I do something that didn't make sense to me?"

I leaned over to refill my glass. Our legs touched.

"Here, let me get it," he said, and he hovered close as he poured it.

I waited.

In his room he ran the errands—pulled the blinds, dimmed the lights, shoved things off the bed—while I took off my necklace, dropping it slowly on the nightstand so the steel wouldn't rattle against the wood. Aware that he was watching me, I tried not to appear curious about his possessions.

My hair got in the way. He caught some of it in his mouth and then it jammed in my zip at the back and he said: "I hope this doesn't end in A&E." "Really," I said, "because I hope it does." "You say the weirdest fucking things," he said.

5

OCTOBER

I couldn't bear living in an Airbnb forever, but I still didn't have a two-month deposit saved. At the start of October, I moved my things to Julian's. I told him I didn't have time to go around viewing places. He said I could stay until I did.

"Take the guest room," he said. "I get calls at night."

We kept having sex.

In mid-October Typhoon Haima came, the last of the season. We were trapped indoors until the Hong Kong Observatory gave the all-clear. Julian wore an unavoidably air-quoted "casual jumper." He called many things casual and kept them in air quotes.

I asked why we'd taken so long to hook up.

"I didn't want to impose," he said.

The answer I'd been hoping for was that I made him nervous. I hadn't thought he'd had the power to "impose," and was startled that he'd felt he had.

His sheets were very white. I once left a blot he called a wine stain, either euphemistically or because he could more readily picture me sipping Merlot than menstruating. His interest in making me come felt sinister at first, which revealed to me my assumption that if he wanted something it would probably harm me. He liked when I bit him but you had to pick your moment and I sometimes thought: there are many things I will never become expert in and I chose this—which did not suggest to me that mine was an internal monologue one would select if one could.

I researched the science of biting, learned it would still hurt him later, and knew exactly how I felt about that information.

He enjoyed when I lampooned men who went for sexual flattery. It confirmed his view that he was not one of them, while ensuring their pet phrases still left my mouth. I'd be picky about menus and he'd say I lacked appetite. "Untrue," I'd say, plus facetious gesture. I felt I'd cracked someone too patrician for the you're-so-good-at-sex spiel, he felt privy to my disdain for men susceptible to the you're-so-good-at-sex spiel, and empirically I sat across the table, ran my foot up his leg, and said he was good at sex. Then I asked for water and watched his hands as he poured.

I wasn't good at most things but I was good at men, and Julian was the richest man I'd ever been good at.

———

Joan often made me stay behind to "help her" write vocabulary lists. In Hong Kong English, "helping someone do something" could mean you did it and they did not assist. Joan was fond of this usage.

That week the twelve-year-olds' list included the word "mind." The dictionary gave four meanings: to be in charge of or deal with; to be offended or bothered by; the seat of the faculty of reason (Iris Huang looked between the chairs); an important intellectual (Iris Huang fixed on a chair).

The dictionary would not equip these children for Dublin. "Mind yourself" upon leaving a house was different to "Mind yourself" when using a serrated knife. "Don't mind him" meant he'd been teasing you, and "Mind him" meant either to take care of him or to take care of yourself around him. And all your minding happened in one mind, hopefully your own.

I was forever minding things in Hong Kong, but I couldn't always construe in what sense.

———

Julian liked being busy. He was so busy, I would say. Just one day I would like to be busier than him. I would like for him to suggest a plan and for me to not be free.

"I'm not that busy," he said. "Why do you want to be busy?"

"It's a status symbol. It's like, 'I'm so in-demand in the skilled economy.'"

"That's not the rich, though. That's people like me."

"But you're rich."

"I'm not."

"You have to stop pretending you don't know you're rich," I said. "It's unbecoming."

Our wealth disparity was too wide to make me uncomfortable. It was a clownish level of difference that I could regard only with amusement. I also felt it absolved me of any need to probe the gendered implications of letting him pay for everything, which was just as well when I couldn't afford for it to be otherwise. If something cost one percent of his income or ten percent of mine, why shouldn't he take care of it?

I googled the salary range for junior vice presidents at his bank: €137,000 to €217,000 a year, plus bonus and housing allowance. I tried to take heart from this. That he could have that many zeroes and not consider himself wealthy surely showed that material lucre would not make me happy, ergo that I needn't find a real job. But if money wouldn't improve my life, I couldn't think of anything likelier to.

Staying in his flat was possibly a rupture from the capitalist notion that I was only worth something if I paid my own way economically. Or maybe it made me a bad feminist. I could puzzle it out once the experience had passed. There wasn't much point in dwelling on it until then. What if I decided I didn't like staying with him? I'd have to do something else, and I mightn't like any of the alternatives any better.

———

Mam always said: "That's plenty." If you tweaked the heating above seventeen—that's plenty, Ava. Grocery shopping, if you made to pick up a second punnet of cherries—that's plenty. I hadn't told Mam I was living with Julian. She'd regard him as more than plenty, which meant too much.

I rang her one weekend when Julian was abroad.

"Any news?" she said, clearing her tone of accusation that I'd only call if there were something to disclose. Mam's genius was that when she avoided implying something, you could hear her doing it.

"Not much," I said.

"How's your one?"

"Your one," unless otherwise specified, meant Joan.

"Grand," I said.

"Your man?"

"Grand."

Benny. The first time I'd told Mam about my employers, she'd said: "They'll keep you out of divilment." In subsequent phone calls she tried to judge how they were doing, and whether they needed help.

"Any fellas?" Mam said.

"Afraid not," I said.

I tried to make it sound like I was looking. Mam had the vague impression that girls in search of boyfriends went to nightclubs, something she liked to picture me, a young one, doing. I could have told her I didn't go because my boyfriend was twenty-eight, but he wasn't my boyfriend and I'd always hated clubbing.

"We've a hard time keeping up with you," Mam said. This comment rarely bore particular relation to whatever I'd just said, but she found it instructive to drop it in.

"How's Tom?" I said.

"He's grand. Did I tell you he's after moving out?"

"Yeah."

"Good lad. Hardworking. Most boys his age you'd need to push out."

She didn't want me to agree that it was good her younger son no longer needed her. Equally, she didn't want me confirming that she should feel defunct because he was leaving before he'd finished college. Mam dealt in conversational quicksands where moving would only trap you more.

(I'd told Julian this and he'd said he never would have guessed that I came from a line of enigmatic women. I'd said: "Why enigmatic women? Why do you think I'm a female-pattern enigma? Maybe the men in my family are enigmatic, too." He'd said: "But you do acknowledge that you're enigmatic." And I'd said: "Maybe, or maybe I was just being enigmatic.")

"George is well," she added. Her listening comprehension deferred to maternal optimism: she assumed that since I'd asked about Tom, I wanted to hear about both brothers. "He's happy with his bonus, did he tell you?"

"He didn't," I said.

He did. George was a corporate restructuring consultant. This mostly entailed helping companies make people redundant without having to give them severance pay. He did a robust sideline in finding ways to avoid granting women maternity leave.

"And they think someone on his team will make senior consultant," Mam was saying. "He's a hard worker—him and Tom. A pair of workhorses."

The word "workhorses" made me think of "workhouses," then of how commodiously situated George would be running one in a Victorian novel. With my college brain on, I knew many more people lost their jobs when banks like Julian's played subprime roulette—but the college brain came with a dial. I turned it up for people I hated, and down for people I liked.

"What about me?" I said. "Am I a workhorse?"

I was trying to be funny, which was an error. You couldn't joke with Mam on a long-distance call.

"You're not getting enough sleep," she said.

—

I liked imagining Julian had a wife back in England. I am a jezebel, I'd think. This wine rack was a wedding gift and I am using it to store Jack Daniel's because I have terrible taste in everything. She is Catholic—in the English recusant aristocrat sense, not the Irish poverty sense—and will never grant him a divorce, and I cannot in any case usurp her as the woman who loved him before life and investment banking strangled him, creatively.

I asked about the wine rack and he said it came with the flat.

I wished Julian were married. It would make me a powerful person who could ruin his life. It would also provide an acceptable reason he did not want us to get too close. The more plausible reading was that he was single and that while I could on occasion discharge the rocket science of making him want to fuck me, he did not want to be my boyfriend. That hurt my ego. I wanted other people to care more about me than I did about them.

As things really stood, I performed petty tasks in exchange for access to him. He jokingly asked me to organize his bookshelf, and when I actually did, he said I was brilliant. From the conditions of the spines I judged that he liked Tennyson, also Nabokov, though they might have been secondhand copies or ones someone else had borrowed. One weekend I made the mistake of pointing out that he should pack for Seoul, and thereafter he expected me to remind him whenever he went on a business trip.

"You're so lazy," I said. "It'd be easier to do it myself than make you do it."

"Knock yourself out," Julian said, which wasn't the response I'd been trying to elicit, but I thought it could be fun, like kitting out a

Barbie doll for an improbable profession. His clothes all looked the same and he kept a toothbrush and shaving things in a travel bag. I didn't include condoms, not because I minded his seeing other people but because I was afraid it would seem passive-aggressive.

I wondered when he spoke to his parents. He alluded to conversations with his mum, but I never heard them talking. Eventually I asked.

"There's a routine," he said. "Every few days, she calls on my lunch break."

"What time is that in England?"

"Six a.m., but she's up. She gardens."

"What about your dad?"

"Hadn't I told you? He's here."

"In Hong Kong?"

"He's a history lecturer at HKU. They divorced when I was ten."

This had only emerged four months into our acquaintance. I wondered what other information he'd been squirreling away, and—God loves a trier—if some of it mightn't be spousal.

"How often do you see your dad?" I said.

"A few times a year. When we manage."

"Where does he live?"

"Three MTR stops away."

"And you see him a few times a year."

"Yes, when we manage."

The English were strange.

Possibly to make fun of me in some obscure way, Julian remembered my parents' names and used them often. "Have you spoken to Peggy recently?" he'd say, or: "How's Joe?" His were called Miles and Florence. I found the comparison illuminating, but he didn't. For Brits, class was like humility: you only had it as long as you denied it.

On the escalator down the next morning I pictured his childhood home in Cambridgeshire. Tall, I thought, and empty: houses were like their owners. (I felt cruel, then decided he'd laugh. This reminded me that nothing I said could hurt him.) Although I was not someone Julian would bring to meet Florence, I imagined her having me for dinner, just the two of us. I'd mispronounce "gnocchi" and she'd avoid saying it all evening so as not to embarrass me. I would meet her eye and think: in this way I could strip you of every word you know. I'd take them like truffles and you'd say, "Help yourself," and then I'd take those, too, and you'd be speechless.

On the journey back up Mid-Levels that evening, I decided it would be very complimentary indeed if Julian were married and not wearing his ring. If he'd worn one, I probably would have taken it to mean he saw me as ambitious.

———

Whenever Julian was abroad, I went drinking with the other teachers. The first time I was invited, Ollie from Melbourne asked: "TST or LKF?" then clarified—Tsim Sha Tsui, Lan Kwai Fong, the nightlife districts—as though this were, including the preschool curriculum, the most obvious thing he'd explained all day. The bars were unlicensed speakeasies, dark and awkwardly spacious, or else rooftops with lights gleaming beyond. During these outings I felt I had hitherto woefully misdirected my energies in attempting to cultivate a personality. If you didn't have one then that left more room for everyone else's.

"Are you seeing someone?" said Briony from Leeds.

"Maybe," I said, four cocktails in.

"Put it another way, are you looking?"

"Maybe."

Then Madison from Texas pulled me into a conversation with two men. Her preferred swain told her she had tits he'd do coke off. There were, as a rule, three sorts of man in TST and LKF: tech, corporate, rugby wolfpack. Madison's pair placed themselves squarely in tech by saying they felt superior to men who wore suits. I felt you could achieve this distinction more efficiently by not having any job. Madison's also-ran touched my arm. I flinched, and he asked if I liked girls. I wanted to say: my chief sexual preference is that I don't like you.

I went to the bathroom and rang Julian. I said: "Do you do coke?"

"What?"

"I've heard all bankers do coke."

———

I'd read that the art critic John Ruskin had been disgusted by an unspecified aspect of his wife's body on their wedding night, which made me realize I'd always had that exact fear about anyone seeing me naked. Julian said kind things about my appearance and all I could say was "Thanks," wishing to be cordial without implying I agreed. I'd feel his arms; wonder (a) why I was a cold and ungrateful person and (b) if anyone would ever love me; know the answers were (a) I'd decided to be and (b) no; and eventually say, "I like your arms."

You could go manless entirely, and I saw a great deal of elegance in that approach, but enough people felt otherwise that I thought it best to have one. You had to pretend to feel sad if you'd been single too long. I hated doing that because there were other things I was actually sad about.

As with not having any man, I felt not having any sex was the decorous option—but if you were going to have it, you should have it with someone who retained a degree of objectivity. And I had to have it. Otherwise I'd never stop thinking. We both preferred me on top and I wondered if that said anything about our dynamic. I felt all your copulative leanings were meant to reveal something deep about you, and if they didn't you had an uncompelling mind.

He wasn't affectionate in bed, but he let me perch my arms on his chest.

"What if I were your age?" I said.

He asked what I meant.

"Would you still be interested in me if I were the same person but your age?"

"How old do you think I am?"

"I don't know," I said, no more conscious of statistics relating to average age of first marriage than any other individual would be. "Thirty?"

"Twenty-eight," he said. "I think I could live with your being twenty-eight as well."

I was disappointed, and realized I'd wanted him to be into the fact that I was twenty-two. There was nothing else I had that he didn't.

Later I googled what anyone would google. I saw twenty-nine for the UK but thirty-one in Hong Kong, reflected that neither statistic said when—or whether—men of his specific socioeconomic bracket and emotional makeup affianced themselves, and with reference to the latter surmised that he was single and did not want me to be his girlfriend. I cried about this no more than any other person would.

6

NOVEMBER

I n November we went for brunch on Aberdeen Street with Ralph, pronounced *Rafe*, who'd gone to Balliol with Julian, now worked at his bank, and had an alleged flotilla of Hibernian great-grandparents. (Two, he expanded. One great-grandparent on each side, which meant Éire owed him a whole grandparent, morally.) He'd voted for Brexit to have tighter borders, and was applying for an Irish passport to avoid being stopped at them. Later in the conversation he called himself "a PPEist" who'd been "a bit of a Union hack." Julian said: "Ralph, you're thirty."

Ralph's girlfriend, Victoria, was good at wearing clothes. She was so beautiful I couldn't see why she was talking to me. Sometimes her eyes said: I don't know why either. We talked and talked, mutually baffled as to why such a thing was happening when neither of us thought it should. Ralph watched us and seemed to think: women are good at talking.

"You're from Ireland," said Victoria, as though for my information. "I've been to Dublin."

"Did you see the Book of Kells?" I said, hoping she'd say no, since I never had. Of course she had not only seen it, but written an extended essay about it for her degree at St. Andrews. Julian disputed her historiography, and she nodded collaboratively as though they were lifting an awkward piece of furniture together from opposite sides. Periodically she touched her Celine trapeze bag. I thought: it's still there, Victoria. It's not going anywhere. The cow's dead.

The following week we drank six bottles of rosé with them in a twenties-style speakeasy. Victoria told me in the bathroom that she was cheating on Ralph with a married hedge-fund guy. She said the thing no one told you about affairs was that the administrative challenges were not inconsiderable. Then she asked if I found it weird that Julian claimed we weren't going out when we clearly were. I said I didn't. "It's weird," she said, authoritatively. She added: "Do you fuck?" which I thought in its own way a remarkable collation of words. She said it with the tone in which one might say, "Do you vape?" another sentence I would never utter. I replied that I did lots of things. "I'm sure you do," she said. Then: "Are those your real eyelashes?"

———

The Hong Kong winter had set in. I called it that, the Hong Kong winter, because I'd have to renounce my Irish passport if I started counting twenty degrees Celsius as actual winter. In truth, I'd been gone nearly five months and did find it cold.

My bank account was growing now, especially from not paying rent. I rarely spent the money. I preferred to think of it as time I could use later.

On the street where I worked I passed tourists eating street food, plodding in and out of scaffolded buildings to haggle in cheap phone shops. The British ones wore shorts, and the wool-coated locals pretended not to see them. There was a small seasonal window where you could dress for winter. It was no one's business spoiling it.

Julian said he'd be in Tokyo in December. I wondered why he was telling me. Then he clarified that it wasn't one of his weekend business trips, but three weeks. I nodded and asked intelligent questions as I separated the rubbish. We'd had dim sum. I took care to rinse the oil off the packaging.

"What are you doing there?" I said.

"Banking. Money."

"Whenever I say you work with money, you're like, Ava, I'm not a retail banker, I'm an investment banker."

"It's all money ultimately," Julian said. "The degree of abstraction is what separates me from the nice man you talk to about getting a credit card. And the level of risk."

"Please, tell me more about how you love black pointy lines and you hate red pointy lines."

"Look, if I could explain my job in a sentence, it wouldn't pay so well."

"Brain surgeons."

"What?"

"Brain surgeons can explain what they do in a sentence," I said. "They fix brains."

"I don't know how I'll manage without these observations in Tokyo," he said. "Keep a diary."

This exchange had catechized Julian on several points. I'd told him that (a) he had a prestigious and well-recompensed job, (b) I didn't, and (c) to break the monotony of his status, he liked women with lip; women other men found waspish, and who found those men feeble, but who were quite at home in his living room—or one of them was, there in archetype and not as someone he specifically cared for, her hauteur being something they had in common.

The blowjob, too, proved edifying.

Men, I could do just fine.

As always, I packed for him, throwing in T-shirts in case he'd be required to flaunt his off-duty fashion sense. I showed him the clothes scrunched up like sushi rolls and said I'd earned a new iPhone at least. "For sure," he said. "I'll come back with a suitcase of Veblen goods." I asked what that meant in English and he said: luxury commodities.

They were different to normal goods in that the demand actually went up with the price.

As he talked, I attended partly to what he was saying and partly to questions such as why I blew him when he did things like say he'd be away for three weeks, which showed he didn't need me; whether I packed for him specifically between blowing him and being bought things so I wouldn't feel him buying me things was directly because I'd blown him; whether, conversely, I did things like pack for him because I was worried he wouldn't buy me things just because I'd blown him and I'd then be forced to confront how little blowing him meant by the only metric he used to show affection; whether the latter was especially bleak because that meant packing for him was worth more than blowing him and I was honestly not that good at packing; and how on earth I emerged from all this convinced I was the powerful one.

I said: "So iPhones are Veblen goods and bread isn't."

"Exactly. Well, bread's a Giffen good. What will you do while I'm gone? I can look up museums."

"I'm not a child. I'll do that myself."

"Just offering."

"Can I come with you?" I said, ironically.

"I'm busy," Julian said, ironically. "It wouldn't be fair on you."

It's never fair, I thought—sincerely. If it were fair then you wouldn't spend so much money on me. The idea came to me fully formed in words before I remembered to be startled by it.

"I know you don't want me to go."

When he said that, I wanted to go to his potentially matrimonial wine rack, choose his jammiest Cabernet Sauvignon, open it tenderly, and empty it over his MacBook. I didn't. He'd buy a new laptop tomorrow, be pleased with the improved touch bar, and deny to my face that I had done that thing with the wine until a point in some future argument where he suddenly needed evidence I was crazy. None of this would address why his comment had upset me.

"Ava, are you all right?" he said.

"I'm fine."

I despised him. Not wanting him to go was an emotion produced by me, not him. He'd witnessed me having and failing to smother a feeling, and said he'd noticed—and he profited, not me. This showed how public-school boys coat-tailed on stolen labor. He receivedly pronunciated his defalcatory fricatives and he took his time doing it, because he could, because he and his vampire class would live forever off lives leeched in their factories and ultimately everywhere else, too, at—smaller words?—some degree of abstraction. My wanting to cry was a reflection mainly of my social conscience.

He opened the window and lit a cigarette.

"Let's talk about something else," I said.

Julian concurred. "Tokyo?"

"Sure. Do you know Japanese?"

"Not a word."

"Konnichiwa," I offered.

"Great, now I've got one word."

"It's actually two. In Japanese. 'Konnichi,' and then 'wa.'"

"Ava, are you all right?"

"I'm fine."

"Listen, I really do like you quite a lot."

"You, too," I said. Which made no sense—surely "You, too" meant I thought he also liked himself a lot—but he didn't mind.

That night I spent longer than usual pretending not to want him in ways that made it obvious I did. It wasn't as much fun as I usually found it, or as satisfying as I knew slicing a machete through a row of his shirts would be, but I enjoyed the clarity of the exercise. There was something Shakespearean about imperious men going down on you: the mighty have fallen.

When we'd finished I borrowed one of his famous casual jumpers and he told me he liked how my ears stuck out. He said it made me look attentive. I asked did he mean I looked like I had good hearing, and he said no, not that exactly, but it made me seem alert.

"In Victorian times," I said, "women cut off a lock of hair and gave it to men to keep."

"I don't want your hair."

"I'm just describing the practice."

"Right. Good description. I still don't want your hair."

"Do you want something else of mine?"

"I've got your texts," he said. "They probably say more about you than your hair. And I want that jumper back."

"I prefer you in a suit," I said.

He didn't sympathize enough with my politics to understand how embarrassing or personal a confession this was.

7

DECEMBER

When Julian and I said goodbye at the airport, I made myself walk away first. I looked up at the steel beams, felt for my suitcase, then remembered I hadn't brought one because I wasn't the one leaving.

In the two months I'd been in the flat, my impression had been that he was hardly around. It turned out he'd been home quite a lot and we often had sex, and I didn't like the sudden withdrawal of these conditions. I didn't want to eat. It felt unnecessary doing it by myself. Alone in the flat, I texted him, but he replied hours later or not at all. I took to calling instead. I felt he could tell from my voice that I was in his bed and wearing his shirt.

At the end of his first week away, I asked on the phone about Japan. He said it was cleaner than Hong Kong, adding that he supposed I read more when he was away.

"In other words," I said, "you think I haven't any friends apart from you."

"You don't need any."

"That sounds like the kind of thing a creepy possessive boyfriend would say."

"It's just as well I'm none of those things, isn't it?"

I wished then that I'd saved my remark for a face-to-face conversation. He sounded weak and studiedly impartial on the phone, like a doctor giving you a negative prognosis near the end of a shift where they'd already delivered lots of other bad news.

"You say that a lot," I said. "'By the way, I'm still not your boyfriend,' like you think I need reminding. I'm not stupid." The statement that I wasn't stupid, which I had intended as neutral information, sounded sharper than expected.

"I'm aware you're not stupid."

"So why do you keep saying it? I feel like you're hiding something."

I didn't really. He'd been clear that he liked having me around but didn't want anything serious. His honesty hurt my pride, so I told myself he was a liar. And I couldn't even feel truly, sumptuously sorry for myself, because it wasn't reciprocation I was craving. My desire was for Julian's feelings to be stronger than mine. No one would sympathize with that. I wanted a power imbalance, and I wanted it to benefit me.

"I don't know why you think I lie about everything," he said.

"Okay, you're not a liar," I said. "Happy?"

"Euphoric. Could you endorse me for that on LinkedIn?"

"I'll get one just to add you."

"I do see how living in my apartment might feel illicit until we've taken that step."

I got out of bed and stood at the door to the balcony.

"Why do you buy me things?" I said.

"Do you mind?"

"No. But I'm curious."

"I mean," he said, "none of it costs very much."

I decided he'd said that on purpose. It was less upsetting than thinking it was accidental.

"If I'm such a scrounger," I said, "you know you can get rid of me."

"Could you rewind to where I called you a scrounger? I seem to have missed it."

"It's the impression I get."

"I can't be held responsible for every tin-hat notion you come up with."

"So I'm a crazy irrational woman."

"If you listen more carefully, Ava, you'll notice I think you're extremely sane. I assume there's some purpose behind what you're saying. I'm trying to unearth what it might be."

"You can't be 'extremely' sane. You're sane or you're not. Like how you can't be 'extremely' allowed to work in Hong Kong."

"As a white British banker, I think it's fair to say I'm extremely allowed to work in Hong Kong."

I laughed. I was always relieved when he said things like that about himself, like: good, so it mustn't annoy him when I do it. People frequently said things about themselves they did not like others saying, but I was not always inclined to be good at men.

"What are we like?" I said.

"I'm not used to dealing with people like you," he said.

Sometimes I was good at him, sometimes he was good at me, sometimes we were good at each other, and sometimes neither of us was any good at anything. The whole thing was so confusing that I wished one of us had all the power and I didn't even care if it was him, though that clearly wasn't true or I'd just let him win—at which point he'd lose interest and replace me with a model because they're thinner or a dachshund because they shed less.

"Are you a dog person?" I said.

"What? No."

"Me neither. I like a bit more of a challenge."

We laughed at men who found such statements gratifying.

"Look," he said, "I'd better go. I've a string of meetings tomorrow. But it was good catching up. Talk soon, babe."

I liked that—babe. It made me feel accounted for.

I went with the other teachers to a bar in TST. We ordered drinks and variously reminded people we were seeing someone or advertised that we weren't. Scott from Arkansas did both. I asked why he was claiming to be single when he'd mentioned his girlfriend three seconds ago, and he said he'd made her up because I intimidated him. I wondered if he would be a better or worse person without narcotics.

In the club down the road, Madison from Texas started dancing with me. We didn't move much but she touched my hip. I remembered in college when a girl was off her face at Workmans and we shifted and a man in a polo shirt asked could he watch. You already are, I'd thought. Men were rarely true voyeurs. They wanted you to know they were there.

Madison said she envied me because I did the inscrutable thing without trying. Men liked that, she said. Madison always thought it would excite me to learn what men liked.

She stroked my arm when Scott from Arkansas approached. Scott said his flatmate was away. Madison said: "That's interesting, Ava, isn't it." There was no limit to what Madison thought would interest me. I asked Scott if he meant his girlfriend was away and whether their arrangement was monogamous, and Madison looked at me like I was a child who'd asked their aunt about her divorce. Narcotics made Scott better, I decided, in that they kept him honest by hampering his ability to lie plausibly.

I wondered what Julian told other women about me.

Madison tried to kiss me. Her tongue tasted cheap, like something from a can.

"You still haven't told me if you like girls," she said.

I said: "There's lots of things I don't tell people."

8

M am thinks there's a guy," said Tom on the phone.

"Why?" I said.

"She says a mother knows and that's how she knows. Circular, but sure look."

He told me about his degree. He was studying philosophy without much gusto, but was getting his essays in and going to lectures and everything. A lecturer had told him he was destined for a mid-2.1, and he wasn't offended like I would have been. Mam kept asking what he'd do after.

"Listen, I've been meaning to tell you," I found myself saying. "Don't tell Mam, but there actually is a guy."

"Okay."

"It's not serious. But it's been good so far. He's posh, though. Not Dublin posh, British posh. He says 'shall.'"

"I'd say you like that," Tom said.

"What's that supposed to mean?"

"Ah now, Ava."

It was true that Julian conformed with my record. My two ex-boyfriends from home had gone to South Dublin private schools and knew all about rugby. (That they had no personal interest in it only made this a clearer mark of status.) It was the sort of theory I could form very easily about someone else: Ava is drawn to wealthy partners as a means of quieting her class anxieties. In practice, having sex with rich people only heightens her awareness that she herself is not rich, and yet she keeps on doing it.

But it felt robotic to conclude something like that about myself. I couldn't help feeling it had to be more complex than that.

"What about you?" I asked Tom.

"There's no one right now," he said. "I'll tell you if there is."

"You always say that. Then three months later, you're like, oh, there was someone but it's over now."

"I don't tell you till I know it's a thing. Then when I do know it's a thing, we break up."

"Do you get a say in it?"

"Sometimes I'm even the one to do it. But I never see it coming. Self-awareness for you."

"You've more of it than me," I said.

"No, you're too self-aware. You can talk yourself into anything. Then there's no talking you out of it."

"Is that why you've not said anything about Julian?"

"Is Julian the Tan?"

"Don't call him a Tan."

"He's still a Tan."

I agreed this was factual.

"Look," Tom said, "I can't tell you what to do."

I wished he would. My stance amounted to: I am glad Julian does not demand intimacy, and annoyed at him for not offering it. I stay in his apartment for free and complain it's done strange things to our dynamic. I hate needing him and address this not by taking responsibility for my own happiness but by playing his games, which could equally be my games because I'm unsure who started it.

I wanted to tell someone that and have them say either: Ava, you are being unreasonable, or: Ava, we all bear our crosses but yours has the most nails. Anything but: sounds complicated.

"I'll let you go," I said.

Tom had more than one person he actually liked seeing.

———

At work I imagined nice things that might happen to me if I were a different person. When I realized I'd been daydreaming, I'd start correctively listing things I disliked about myself. The children wrote essay plans and I thought: flat feet, doughy hands, clumsiness, moral cowardice. When Matthew Yim asked a question, I felt rudely interrupted. The poster opposite said PREPOSITIONS OF MOVEMENT. It had frogs in different locations: on the table, under the table. I thought: pale, hostile to people who have shown me nothing but kindness, probably bad at sex.

In the staffroom the others were talking about adopted versus biological children. I said: "I'd adopt. I wouldn't inflict my gene pool on anyone."

"Aw, don't say that about yourself!" said Madison from Texas.

To the list I added: sense of humor not for everyone.

———

Three weeks into December, the day before Julian's return, I messaged him.

> hey so i want to say sorry for how i've been treating you. i'm really unnecessarily mean to you and i justify it as socialist praxis when it literally isn't. i don't want to call myself a horrible person bc i know i do that so you can't say it. but i like having you in my life.

I sent it on the balcony. If I threw my phone over the railings, I'd never see if he replied. The patio in front of the lobby looked like a small mosaic tile from overhead. Ant-people played out their personal histories with the same degree of immersion that I was experiencing mine.

Julian replied a few hours later.

Thanks for the message. I know it can't have been easy to write. I'll see you soon.

It could have meant anything, including what it purported to.

I surprised him at the airport. The arrivals section was huge, but his height made him easy to spot. At passport control he had everything ready so as not to waste time. He met my eye from far away. I ran to meet him.

anking slowed down just before Christmas. I suspected Julian told me that with disapproval. His MD had darkly intimated he'd be pleased with his bonus, which meant top tier or none at all. "Hengeveld's a sadistic American cunt," Julian said, "so quite possibly the latter." He made no financial plans that relied on the money, then found himself perplexed what to do with it. I said that must be hard for him.

"What's 'American' doing in that sentence, by the way?" I said.

Julian took off his suit jacket and placed first it and then himself on the couch, like: pray, elaborate.

I said: "You seem more resentful when your superiors are American."

Julian explained there was an important difference. When an American MD wanted something on their desk tomorrow morning, they said they wanted it on their desk tomorrow morning. When a British one did, they said it wasn't urgent; tomorrow morning would do.

That evening I made us try cooking, phrasing it that way—I am making us try cooking—so Julian would see it as a cultural activity, like ceramics classes. He chopped the vegetables and remarked that he'd do it professionally if it paid better than banking. I asked if there was anything he wouldn't do for more money, and he said no, probably not.

"I should mention," he said, "that I'll have to see my father."

"That's fairly common," I said. "At Christmas."

"It's just that if I have to spend Christmas with Miles and you want to spend Christmas with me, that means both of us will need to go."

"I don't mind," I said. "I'd love to meet him."

"He'll like you. He hates 'neoliberalism,' though I've never heard him define it."

I laid out the cutlery and wineglasses. After dinner, he read one of his Victorian doorstoppers and encouraged himself to quit smoking by finishing off a Chinese cigarette pack he termed "particularly vile." I looked at things on my phone and balanced my mental energy between (a) speculating as to whether his father's politics suggested there was a degree of daddy issues bound up in his attraction to me, and (b) concealing this normal and healthy thought process from Julian. That was what we did. We were the sum of the routines we'd built around each other.

———

Joan told me to teach the kids about Christmas in Ireland. Hearing my description, I began to doubt it was something my family actually did. I said people went to the tree shop and bought a tree, and felt it was probably all lies.

The children weren't curious. Joan was always saying to throw in my value-added, to tell them things a local teacher couldn't. But none of the differences mattered. Sometimes it snows at Christmas, I said, but more often it doesn't. People jump in the sea. It's very cold. But it's getting warmer, as it is everywhere, and probably within our lifetimes the oceans will rise and drown us.

In each class that week, the center of attention was whoever was going furthest away for the break—Mary Yeung to Bangkok, Hsu Chung Sun to Sydney, Emmeline Fan to New York. Some were visiting family. Others were obeying the ever-robust principle that one could not expect rich people to stay anywhere too long.

As we closed shop that evening, Joan ranted about a mother from Beijing who'd wanted the leaflets about the classes available in simplified Chinese as well as traditional. She chewed fish balls from a bamboo skewer between sentences. Seeing a chance to bond, I told Joan there'd been similar debates over Irish-language orthography. She put down her bowl and asked which we used now. I said we'd simplified, and Joan resumed gnawing. She held many grievances against mainland China. The ones concerning Hong Kong's political autonomy were compelling, and the ones about tourists less so.

On the last day before term break, she told me to call my mother on Christmas Day.

"I will," I said.

"It's important."

"You're right, Joan."

"Mothers are important."

"They are."

10

Miles and the waiter chatted in Cantonese. Every now and then, Miles pointed at one of us and Julian refreshed the email on his phone.

It was Christmas Eve. We'd met in the lift lobby on Percival Street. There were thirty floors and at least as many restaurants in the tower. The place we went to had dark wood paneling, paper screens, and round mahogany tables. Miles's conversation with the waiter had started with coordinating to find vegetarian options for me, though I suspected they'd moved off that topic.

"He'd never spend that long talking to locals," said Julian after the waiter left. "He's showing he's got a way with gweilos."

"Or perhaps he was being friendly," Miles said. He was sixty-three, Julian had said. Like his son, he favored shirts. Unlike Julian's, they were pinstriped and needed ironing.

On the train over, Julian had told me not to mention our relationship. "Just don't say anything," he said. "It won't be the only proboscidean in the room." I'd said: "Why don't you tell him? And then that's one less elephant, if 'proboscidean' is some pretentious Latin joke." Julian said: "I don't want him knowing. And actually, 'proboscidean' is a pretentious taxonomy joke." I'd said: "But you said he already knows." And Julian had replied: "Right. I'm okay if he knows. I just don't want him knowing."

Clever about Latin, clever about taxonomy, able in his intellect to brook being called pretentious provided you matched his penchant for scathing women. I didn't take holidays. I also found the phrase "his penchant for scathing women" interesting, grammatically. It did sometimes strike me that one could equally say Julian had, e.g. managed things so he could take me to meet his father and still make it about how detached he was, detachment being something he knew I both wanted and didn't want from him and which he played up to these conflicting levels of desire as, respectively, carrot and stick—but historians could debate all that when we were dead and interesting.

The waiter came back with three glasses of hot water. "Tell me, Ava," Miles said, "what do you make of the election?"

"In Hong Kong?" I said.

"Yes, yes, for the chief executive in March."

"Stop grilling her," Julian said. "They're all mainland puppets anyway."

I should have been grateful, but wasn't. Did he think I couldn't handle Miles? As it happened, I couldn't name a single candidate, but Julian didn't know that about me.

"All right, how about you, Julian?" said Miles. "Lam or Tsang? Since heaven knows you won't be backing the underdog."

"Untrue. I was with Blair till the end."

"And against Corbyn from the beginning."

"I will readily admit to a prejudice against having dangerous nutters lead parties."

"Spare a thought for me, Ava," Miles said. "The one thing worse than a centrist dad is a centrist son."

"How much does your university pay its cleaning staff, Miles?" Julian said.

"Shamefully little," Miles said. "It would almost suggest that capitalism doesn't fairly remunerate socially important labor."

"I wonder which creates more jobs—my directing capital where it will stimulate the most growth, or your writing books about how this makes me a bourgeois parasite."

"Certainly the books. Hordes of *Guardian* writers keep the wolf from the door by pretending to have read them."

"Whereas I do it for free," said Julian. "Maybe I'm the communist."

Miles turned to me. "What brings you to Hong Kong, Ava?" he said.

I said: "I'm here to teach." I tried to balance my chopsticks on top of the bowl, then noticed a small wooden rest for them. I never knew what to do when someone had obviously asked me a question to include me in the conversation. How much could I say in response before I was abusing their generosity?

Miles said: "Teach what?"

"English."

"Tell her what you think about Ireland," Julian said. "She'll like that."

"First," Miles said, "I'd like to hear what you think I think about Ireland."

Julian said: "Isn't it that independence was a waste of time because the free state hasn't yet transitioned to full communism?"

"I appreciate the 'yet.' But I don't know that that was my precise contention. I do think the republic has betrayed the socialist contingency that fought for it."

"When should we have left?" said Julian. "Everywhere the British left later than Ireland, it was too late for you, and yet Ireland was too early."

"When did I say Ireland was too early?"

"You don't like what happened after we left. The only counterfactual is staying longer."

Miles blew on his tea. "The fact that you consider that the only counterfactual," he said, "tells me all I need to know about the history faculty at Oxford."

"I think I picked up my ideological stubbornness from a slightly earlier influence," said Julian.

They stopped talking about politics for a while after that.

———

The flat was cold when we got back. I turned on the heater and wrapped up in one of the throws. Julian asked what I'd made of Miles. I said I liked him.

"I'm not trying to turn you against him," said Julian, "but I think you should know that my parents divorced because he had an affair."

He wouldn't want me to say anything sympathetic, so I didn't. His shoes looked scuffed. I told him to leave them by the couch so I could polish them tomorrow.

"Why did he send you to Eton?" I said.

I considered it a deviant thing for any parent to do to their child, but a Marxist one especially.

"That was Florence," Julian said. "A key boiling point. Florence thought Miles wanted to, quote, sacrifice her son's education on the altar of socialism. Miles felt Florence wished to, quote, seal me in a hermetic bourgeois bubble. It was especially fraught because we were entitled to bursaries and Miles thought it was outrageous that we'd take the money from somebody who actually needed it."

And now I knew all about his family life, he said. As much as he did, anyway, which he suspected was relatively little of it.

I knew that was the kind of disclosure he'd instantly regret making, so I didn't ask him to unpack it.

11

On Christmas Day, Julian went to church with Miles. I stayed in bed and phoned my family. When he returned, presents: necklace for me, wallet for him—the things you gave colleagues in gift exchanges when you wanted them to know you'd gone over the spending limit. It was the first time I'd bought him something. I couldn't help thinking I should have asked permission.

Ralph and Victoria threw a Christmas dinner. Their flat had big white rooms, a long glass table, and, remarkably, enough friends to fill it.

Victoria passed around duck canapés and said it was a shame Seb—Slaughters, was it, or Linklaters—and Jane—J.P. Morgan or Morgan Stanley—couldn't make it, but lucky them, having time to fly home. From this we understood that Ralph and Victoria were more important than Morgans who slaughtered and linked later, that we were, too, or we'd be with our relatives and not in Hong Kong, and that if Seb and Jane were in the country, they'd have come. You could tell the festive spirit had taken Victoria from her encompassment of us, her guests, in her claims about who was busiest. Alternatively, you could be me and not have had money for flights home.

I didn't take a canapé. "Being good, Ava?" Victoria said. Her implied temporality spoke volumes.

"I'm a vegetarian," I said.

Victoria had large teeth. They made it difficult for her to smile without scaring people, which was why Victoria smiled a lot.

After dinner everyone pretended it was the loud sort of Christmas party you have the week before. It was easier than acting like family. Ralph put on a jazz playlist, and at each new song told all who were curious it was a pity the artist had died young.

Victoria ushered me over to her "other" Irish friend, as though she'd had each of us imported at the other's request. "One of yours, Oisín," she said, and he looked at her like she'd handed him adoption papers penned in crayon. He soon mentioned he'd gone to Gonzaga. He was a rich Irish person, preferred having wealth in common with Victoria to Ireland in common with me, and was annoyed at us both for disabusing him that Victoria saw it that way. His mouth said it was great to see another Mick out foreign, and his eyes said: don't fuck this up for me.

As a buffer I drew in two Englishmen I knew from previous events. Oisín could like me then. The three of them did, and I'd had enough wine to pretend I liked them, too. Someone said Julian had called me "very bright." I felt an impulse to run over, look up at Julian, and go: very bright, saying it like I was drinking Victoria's wine—relishing not having paid for it. Then I'd stay in his pocket forever. I was able to fill in "considering," but chose to stay dizzy on the first two words.

Victoria had left us and joined Julian by the window. She was giggling and doing most of the talking, so I gathered she was laughing at her own jokes.

I couldn't go over. He'd think I missed my owner.

In groups Julian talked quietly and slowly. Really his calm insouciance betrayed as much entitlement as Ralph's braying—more, since he made you listen harder—but it was soothing. I usually spoke softly, too, and sometimes thought: a little lower and no one can hear us.

"She was blotto," Victoria yelled.

I wondered if Victoria was a real person or three Mitford sisters in a long coat.

"Was she," Julian said.

The men around me talked about their schools. As an adult with a job, I did not find the topic altogether piquant—but British men were resourceful, and found school not only interesting, but the most interesting thing they'd ever done. Andrew had been to Radley, and Giles to Manchester Grammar. Giles joked that they were similar schools, which was how I learned Andrew's was better. They reminisced about rugby. Oisín contributed so they'd know Gonzaga played, too. Max joined, waited, then unsheathed: Westminster.

I was outside their figurations. No one asked where I'd gone.

"Will we do some white?" Oisín said.

An English person would have said "shall," but he was understood.

I declined. Julian wouldn't like it. He did coke on occasion, but said I had an addictive personality. I was too pleased with "very bright" to hold this against him at the party, so I mentally stored it for the next time I hated him and lacked a sensible reason. Controlling what women do with our bodies, I thought, preparatively. The men started cutting and I went to the toilet. Coming back, I bumped into another man who looked at me, muttered "Julian's"—as one might say: "chair," or: "floral arrangement"—and stumbled on.

In the red taxi home I described the man. The driver had seven phones of assorted vintage plugged into the dashboard. Julian saw me looking and explained they were for queuing dispatches. I could tell he was drunk because he said my name slowly and when I held his hand he scrunched our fingers tighter. Then he said: "Was that Chris Marshall?" I said I didn't know. Julian said it had to be Chris Marshall, that every woman had a Chris Marshall story, and that at least mine didn't feature hands. I asked why Chris was asked to things if he was, best-case scenario, a contactless creep, and Julian said he'd gone to Habs with Will and Bristol with Ellie, so they couldn't very well leave him out.

Few of those nouns meant anything to me, but I'd had no invitations of my own.

We had sex the next morning and for a while I felt safe and warm and understood. I scratched him a lot, he called me a tiger cub, and I pretended to find it infantilizing because it made me so happy. Unusually, he stroked my hair. He said everyone had liked me at Victoria's. I wondered if he was being nice because (usual reason) his friends wanted to fuck me, (holiday special) I was lonely enough to not only spend Christmas with terrible people but be glad they'd tolerated me, or (clever girl) I'd come faster than usual and he believed in positive reinforcement. I wanted to tell him that in a framework where affection was circumspect, its overt forms were necessarily hostile. Look, I'd say, it's like English grammar. It doesn't make sense but it's too late to change it. When you buy me clothes it means you want to stroke my hair, so when you really stroke my hair it means you want me to move to Siberia and die.

Then he said he'd head to the airport. He had meetings in Bangkok. I asked how anyone could expect him to go, and he said if restaurant staff worked Christmas Eve then surely he could do Boxing Day. "St. Stephen's Day," I said, and he said, no, Boxing Day. I said he was wrong. He said I was wrong. I nearly asked him to stay, but could feel the demand grow in me to never leave this bed and I won't either, which was not a program he seemed apt to endorse, so I didn't.

12

JANUARY 2017

The next week Julian took a cab from the airport to meet me at Admiralty station. He wore a suit. I had a black dress on, so we looked like a particularly drab pair of twins. We walked to the LockCha Tea House, passing fountains and manicured hedges in Hong Kong Park. I asked how things were in Thailand. My voice made me sound like someone who often had occasion to wonder.

"Trundling along," he said. "A lot of people are still in mourning for the king."

We stood outside the door while he finished his cigarette. I said I wanted to quit my job.

"Good," he said. "They aren't paying you enough."

"It's not about money." I went to crack my knuckles, then remembered that was bad for you. "I'll start paying rent."

"Don't worry about that, but you need a plan."

He stubbed out the cigarette, like: here's mine, for instance.

Inside there was a checklist menu where you ticked what you wanted. Julian encharged me with the pencil. I felt this implied it was his by default. We chose huai shan and wolfberry seed soup, yellow cucumber salad, bean curd dumplings, and sticky rice wrapped in lotus leaves. Our green tea arrived, then dim sum.

"I still don't know what I want to do," I said. "I mean in the long term."

"What about teaching? If you got qualified, it mightn't be so bad at a real school."

"It takes too much out of me," I said.

You were supposed to find it endearing that children thought only of themselves. Especially if you were a woman, it was meant to make you want one of your own. It would do parents a world of good if I told them their child actually suffered from a form of self-absorption that some adults outgrew and others didn't. They could note the risk factors: only child, male only child, privately educated male only child whose parents, at odds with their stated politics, gave that child everything until he was of an age to buy it all himself, fellatio potentially included depending on how I was feeling about my own motives. But none of this seemed quite the rub for term reports.

"My dream job is proofreading," I told Julian. "Do banks need proofreaders?"

"The analysts do it."

"Maybe I could be one."

"It's not all they do. They're flunkies. Half of it is stuff it's quicker to do myself, but you can't do grunt work once you're more senior. It looks out of place."

"There's the famous efficiency of capitalism."

"That comment was distinctly Milesian. Eat your soup."

Julian often reminded me to eat. It made him feel better about liking that I was thin.

We navigated the dim sum. It was meant to be eaten with everything shared in the center, but some of it wasn't to Julian's liking, so we sectioned off dishes for individual consumption. He said he didn't mind that there was no meat, but they ought to have something with protein in its place. I pointed out the bean curd and he said he meant something that wasn't made of soy.

When we'd finished eating, Julian said: "I remember the first time

I saw you. You were walking so carefully in your heels. I was wondering what this shy person was doing having so much hair."

"That's a good line. Did you prepare it in advance?"

"There were several drafts. I struck out a few commas on the flight back."

"I don't have that much hair," I said. "Not compared to Victoria. And most people don't think I'm shy anymore."

"That's true. Seb thinks you're, quote, vivacious."

"I feel like 'vivacious' is one of those words where you're not literally calling someone sexy, but everyone knows you are. Which one is Seb again?"

"Scruffy hair. Litigation."

"Dreamy Seb. I did wonder about that friend request."

We were happy then. Julian had complimented both my outer sparkle and the interior layer only clever people saw. We knew I was complex when others didn't. This made us better, or at any rate different, which because of our contempt for them still made us better. The cherry: we were attractive—me because dreamy Seb liked me and Julian because why would someone dreamy Seb liked be with someone less dreamy than dreamy Seb—while Julian's abetment assured us we were conducting an ultimately shallow emotional transaction in which "dreamy" featured. Throughout Julian spoke to me the way an aloof person would want to be addressed, which told me I'd convinced him, if not myself, that I was one. And I returned the favor.

We didn't always volley well, but when we did it was magic.

"By the way," I said, "Victoria's into you."

"Too much hair."

As with any backhand game, when pros played pros it looked easy.

I knew where we stood. Good people supposedly wound up with money, and I wanted to be good, so Julian's zeroes felt summative. This was different to thinking he was or we were. I ate my soup.

On the walk back he offered me a cigarette. I said I had enough problems without adopting his just for company. "Company for your

other problems or company for me in my nicotine dependence?" he
said, and I said: "Get fucked," smiling to remind him this was Irish for
warmth. I felt protective when he smoked. This made no sense when
he was jeopardizing my lifespan, but I supposed he was endangering
his own even more.

Sometimes I thought I'd outlive him by decades. I'd explain him
then. Men wore suits at the time, I'd say. They earned more than
women. In Ireland you got five years for rape, fourteen for aborting
your rapist's fetus, and a lifetime in the laundries for the fact of being raped, and there was a laundry still open when you were born.
None of this was directly the fault of the men you fucked but it influ-
enced how you went about fucking them, especially in Dublin where
you might need to ask them for money. No one could start having sex
with that calculation in mind and not have it affect them wherever
they went, though not all women responded quite so unsubtly as by
fucking bankers.

There were other reasons you liked him, some actually quite pure,
e.g. his dry humor and his shared assessment that you were both a
great deal smarter than anyone else you knew. All couples thought
things like that about themselves, but you hoped for their sake that
the rest of your relationship was nothing they saw in their own, because you didn't want to identify with most of it and you were one half
of that actual couple. Mathematically if you didn't want to be "most"
of a couple, as in over fifty percent of an entity of two, then that did
not commend your practice of self-love. You were twisted individu-
als successfully mated, like Noah's Ark for sociopaths. Alternatively,
you were well-meaning albeit imperfect humans with uncommonly
scarce emotional resources at their disposal. Spending money and
being good at men came easier than real generosity.

There was more to your performative detachment than just the
Eighth, but it stayed with you after you left Ireland. You were afraid
when men came in you, though you were unsure if that was all Irish
women or just you, and sometimes you'd say do you want to finish

in my mouth because after all this you still felt you owed him somewhere. When you came yourself, you feared against all biology that it might be what sentenced you. You knew if you told him any of this he'd understand just enough to break his heart, but seeing how little he could comprehend before it broke him would break you, too. You were ironical with him, also with yourself. It was wild.

13

A few days into January, work started again. Madison from Texas greeted me by launching into a description of her new-year new-me fitness regimen. "I'm going to be me, but worse," I said.

"I think I'm getting the hang of you," she said, then laughed theatrically. But I hadn't been joking.

I was quieter and more openly begrudging now, and it was becoming clearer than ever that the other teachers found me odd. I'd encountered this opinion so many times, in so many places, that I'd come to find it comforting. It doesn't matter if a fact is good or bad, I thought. You don't mind once everyone agrees. Their consensus makes it true, and truth feels safe.

The main thing they considered weird was how I spent my lunch breaks. I'd leave, taking care not to steal minutes, and come back just on time. The staffroom wall was thin. I heard Scott from Arkansas say, where's she going? I alternated between Starbucks and Pacific Coffee in the hope that the baristas would never come to recognize me. None of this seemed outlandish. But my colleagues' muttering made me feel that probably they were right and the whole thing did show I was in some way faulty.

Victoria also found me odd. On weekends we cast around for topics of shared interest while the men discussed things like England beating Wales. (Julian described the result as "pivotal; cardinal, even," to a round of nods, and later told me he believed, but wasn't sure, that the sport had been rugby.) When she was drunk, we went to the bathroom. She liked looking in the mirror. She had a lot of hair. Posh girls had more than I did, but often enough it was from someone else's head.

"I'd fuck Julian," she said one Saturday night.

I said: "Okay."

I wondered if her scalp got itchy with strangers' hair glued to it.

"Do you think he'd fuck me?" she said.

"I don't know. Maybe."

"You must have some take on it."

I held my palms open as though cradling an opinion I couldn't see but the weight of which I felt. "I told you," I said, "I don't know."

"He's never tried to fuck me," Victoria said. "I don't know if he would."

"I'm not the best person to ask."

"You're fucking him. That must give you some indication of who else he'd fuck."

"No," I said, "it really doesn't."

She told me it was sad Julian and I weren't a couple. Kat seemed a difficult person to get over. When he was ready, he'd find someone. I was kind to bridge the gap.

I wondered if I pulled her hair, would the bits that were hers stay in place and would only the extensions from other heads come out, or would it all break off if I tugged hard enough.

━━━

The skies were thick and bronchial. Joan had said to cover my head when it rained or I'd get acid on my scalp. She claimed the bad chemicals blew in from China, but you smelled them coming out of lorries and idling buses on the street. I downloaded an app to check the air quality each morning. A happy face meant it was safe, a blank one that the health risks were moderate, and an angry one to stay inside. After seven consecutive angry faces, I deleted the app. I did not need that negativity in my life.

Julian asked if I missed home. I told him not all Irish people were parochial.

"It's normal to miss your family," he said.

I said that was why I didn't.

The trouble with my body was that I had to carry it around with me. In train stations I picked around other feet like brambles. Rats, too, lived low. Julian said it was good we were on a high floor because cockroaches couldn't reach it. But you had to go down every day to be a part of things.

From his flat halfway up the mountain I saw high-rises like saw-edged computer parts, noxious trees—virescent, not green—and squares leveled for tennis courts. I looked out my window and told myself: it is fair enough to find it stressful that my entire life revolves around someone who does not care very much about me. This is a permissible experience.

—

Despite hating my job and complaining about it often, I still hadn't quit. Julian told me to relax. I told him I'd pay back all the rent I owed and he said not to bother. I'd be better off saving a deposit on a mortgage. He kept meaning to do that himself.

"Now this is just my personal take," I said, "but maybe it would help if you accepted money when people offer it."

"If you want to pay me rent, go ahead."

Between sentences he typed on his laptop. Talking to me demanded so little of him that he'd get bored if he gave it his full attention. I knew

I loathed him—not least because I was fully aware that if he told me to jump off a bridge, I'd say: Golden Gate or Sydney Harbour?—but I now wondered if I mightn't also hate him.

"Is something wrong, Ava?"

"Do you want me to depend on you?" I said. "So you can have more power in the relationship."

"I don't know that anyone has power in this relationship. Either of us could leave it very easily, so it can't be that much of a vise-grip, can it?"

"But I can't leave easily. I'd need to find somewhere to stay."

"I suppose," he said.

I couldn't tell if he was bluffing about not caring if I left. The fact that he could plausibly bluff was already bad enough. Who would believe me if I said it made no difference whether I lived in his apartment or a dingy Airbnb? Yes, I'd say, I am perfectly apathetic as to whether I spend most of my income renting a tiny room with people who hate me. These things are quite subjective. I could have soft towels and five-star dinners, or I could check my windowsill every morning to see how many cockroaches died there in the night. You see it's one or the other and there's no accounting for taste.

I told him he wasn't always nice to me. He asked for even one example. I said that sort of reaction was exactly what I meant.

"You're not Saint Francis of Assisi yourself," he said.

"Would you look at me when you say things like that."

"I don't want to fight."

"It wouldn't be a fight if you'd look at me."

"Forget it, Ava."

"You can't just say that and then expect me not to say anything back."

"I said you are not Saint Francis of Assisi. You manage, somehow, to find that claim controversial."

"Why are you so patronizing?"

"Some people lend themselves to it."

I went to his bookcase and touched the cracks in the spines. They evidenced where he'd lingered, corroborated no doubt by fingerprints. I wondered where in the flat I'd shed DNA. Not on his laptop, because that was important, but onto everything in the kitchen, and his clothes from ironing them and his bedroom carpet from kneeling on it. Men. My cells were on the books, too, but only from tidying. I'd never read the authors he admired. He'd laugh if I tried. Probably he laughed in his head every time I said anything.

"Would you mind sulking somewhere else?" Julian said. "I have a presentation tomorrow."

"It's my flat, too."

"I suppose my credit cards are yours as well. Since your definition of owning something is that you use it and don't pay me back."

"I'll pay you rent. I want to pay you rent."

"I don't know what you want," he said.

We didn't speak for six days. I stayed in my room to avoid him, which meant I couldn't eat and had to drink water from my bathroom sink. My paycheck was late. I'd put money away from staying in the flat for free but had thought of it as an emergency fund, which made using it feel scary. Still I wasted it with mechanical rigor, buying coffees back to back and noting to the cent how much they'd cost. This was apparently the future I'd been saving for.

I also went to malls, as if to say: he thinks he's so clever, buying me things, when in fact I can also buy me things. In Topshop I tried on sickly synthetics and thought: these clothes are both hideous and necessary. It reminded me of shoplifting as a teenager. I'd fill my pockets, go home, lay out the movables on the bed, and think: why did I risk a criminal record for purple lipstick? It does nothing for my complexion.

Mam texted asking how I was. I typed: i am very unhappy. Autofill offered three different negative emojis. I tapped one and it replaced the word "unhappy" with a sad face. Then I deleted the draft and sent one saying I was grand.

On the seventh day, I apologized to Julian. He said it was fine.

14

I looked on flatshare sites. In late January I went to viewings. One room, for half my salary, was the lounge. Not a separate one: the room you entered when you opened the front door. The flatmates explained that the rent was so low because they understood how the arrangement might compromise my privacy—though they noted there was a curtain to pull around the bed at night. They demonstrated how to draw it. I felt the mechanics were not the main objection, but gamely tried. Two hours later, they texted saying the previous girl they'd shown around had just taken the room—so sorry, but the market moves fast.

I thought of Emily and Freya, and my stale mouth in the morning when I couldn't brush my teeth. The smell in my old room, too: the damp laundry, and something portentous from the cracks in the walls. Sometimes in bed, hiding from my flatmates, I'd stared at the fault lines till they started to spread. I saw the walls collapse and heard the screams.

A few days after I apologized, when it was very late and very dark, Julian said he'd been lonely before I came to live with him. He didn't always feel like drinking, and there wasn't much else his friends enjoyed. And you couldn't have proper conversations in groups. He liked having someone at home.

"Shame it's you," he added. I supposed he had to.

My eight-year-olds had mastered prepositions and were now on question words. We recited them like bullets: who what when where why. Most English people said "what" as "wot," though authors only spelled it "wot" when the characters were poor. Sometimes I said "wot," but with my parents I pronounced it as they did: "hwot." This had been correct when Churchill said it but was hokey now so Cameron did not. Even the Queen had stopped haitching it, at the behest, no doubt, of some mewling PR consultant. Irish English kept things after Brits dropped them. "Tings" was incorrect, you needed to breathe and say "things," but if you breathed for "what" then that was quaint. If the Irish didn't aspirate and the English did then they were right, but if we did and the English didn't then they were still right. The English taught us English to teach us they were right.

I was teaching my students the same about white people. If I said things one way and their live-in Filipino nanny said them another, they were meant to defer to me. Francie Suen's mother thanked me once for my hour a week. I smiled, accepted her praise, and never asked whether she should also credit the helper who spoke English with Francie every day. From job adverts on expat forums I estimated she made a quarter of what I did. One forum post asked what children should call their helpers. The parent knew "auntie" was common but worried that if they called the helper that and later fired them, the kid would think other family members could also be dismissed.

On days off it was illegal for helpers to stay in the house. This was so the government knew they were really getting a holiday. They didn't have the money to go other places indoors, so they sat on cardboard boxes in parks and on walkways.

The parents took sixteen hours a day from their helpers, then complained if I started lessons three minutes late. When Joan accused me of stealing time, I thought: yes, and so do bosses.

People on Instagram posted quotes about relationships. They paired them with landscapes and tourist snaps. In white block capitals, next to a mountain goat: CHASE DREAMS, NOT PEOPLE. Over the Kremlin: I WANT A BOY WHO KISSES ME LIKE I'M OXYGEN.

Since the fight, I took stock when Julian did things that made me happy. He laughed at my jokes and I noted: he recognizes that I am capable of irony. Irrationally, because I was not special, I felt he was the only person who would ever understand me.

"You're so pale," he said.

"Sorry."

"It's a compliment."

"Sorry."

I wondered if anyone had liked me in Dublin. Mam, Tom, arguably Dad. In college people had liked that I could roll cigarettes—despite not smoking—and that I didn't interrupt them when they talked about *Infinite Jest*. Admittedly that was because I hadn't read it, but nor had they. I'd thought about reading it but felt my doing so would upset everyone a great deal. The men there said they liked girls who didn't wear makeup in the tone in which less enlightened men said they liked girls who did, and when you actually wore none they asked if you'd been ill. They lamented not having "permission to write." You had to nod, like: oh, to be permitted.

At least Julian was honest. He'd never experienced anything but permission, I hated him for it, but all the same I was glad he knew he had it. Most men with permission never realized.

When he was late home I texted: i'm bored can we fuck. He'd ring me to say he was busy. He liked ringing and saying he was busy. "I'm busy," he said. "And you have a low boredom threshold."

"That objection doesn't betray much sexual confidence on your part."

"I thought you said sexual confidence in men was repulsive."

"No, you said your anarchist ex at Oxford thought that and you suspect I agree."

"Charlie. She was hot."

"I know. I found her profile."

"She went both ways," he said. "Should that interest you. Anyway, I'm busy."

"And I'm bored."

After he came home and fucked me, I went to my own room and revisited the daydream about dining with his mother, mispronouncing words to gag her from saying them. I'd go around all the sinks and turn on the taps, wait, then watch her inch her feet up.

15

FEBRUARY

Anything strange?" said Mam on the phone. She really said it "antin strange," but if Brits spelled Glosster as Gloucester then I supposed Mam deserved similar leeway.

She told me George had a new girlfriend. "The top of her hair is brown, but the bottom is orange. What do you call it?"

"Ombre."

"Amber," she repeated diligently. "And what about the fella?"

"What fella?"

"Tom was telling me. The banker fella."

"He's well," I said. "It's not serious."

"And he'd work for a bank now?"

I said that yes, bankers tended to.

"Good man. They say you become the people you're surrounded with."

"So if a white collar hasn't physically sprouted out from my neck by this time next year, the relationship will be a failure."

"You say such funny things," Mam said. This was different to her saying she thought I was funny. "When are we meeting the banker fella?"

"Let's not get ahead of ourselves," I said. "Hey, Mam, did I tell you he works in a bank?"

"I'll let you go now. Tell the banker I said hi."

"Bye, Mam," I said. As she said goodbye back, I interrupted: "Wait, Mam, I can't believe I forgot to say: he's a banker."

She hung up.

It was February 2, Julian's birthday. He went for drinks with friends. He asked me along but said I would probably not enjoy it, which I decided meant he didn't really want me there. He smelled of smoke when he got back. I wondered if the cheap Chinese cigarettes were really to encourage him to quit smoking, or me to quit him—and why neither strategy was working. I made him tea and gave him a Ferragamo tie with a tiger cub pattern. It was a suitable choice in that he was a man and men wore ties, and also, I supposed, in that it referenced something he'd said in bed. Still I worried. As with the wallet, he might take it to mean I thought him buying me things was about intimacy.

"I thought you should have something," I said. My wording elided that I was the one giving him it.

"You shouldn't spend your money on me," he said.

The phrase "thank you" was available to most English speakers, including the toddlers I taught. He'd heard it quite often enough from me to be familiar with its usage.

Later I asked if there were things he aimed to achieve before turning thirty.

"No," he said. "I've just got vice president and the next rung is managing director, which they're not going to make me. And I'm not here for good, so there's no point in buying an apartment. Couldn't afford it anyway."

I asked if there was anything else. He said no. He didn't see it as a landmark.

That was fine. I did not probe further on whether he, e.g. saw us still together then, or e.g. had ever loved anyone. Really it was amusing that we were having sex. He was attractive and confident, whereas I was willing to center my emotional life around someone who treated me like a favored armrest—and yet there we were, fucking. Funny, the choices we made. There were people in the world that Julian did not want to have sex with. This meant he valued me above them in at least one capacity, a hilarious miscalculation given that I was in fact the worst human on any conceivable axis. And actually, it was even funnier that we were just fucking than it would have been if he'd had feelings for me. I was pathetic enough to seem emotionally endearing, but you would have to be genuinely depraved to look at me and literally just think: I want to exchange fluids with her. So I didn't want him to love me. I was having too much fun for that.

Benny was not taken with my post-Christmas surliness. He liked to remind me that the demand for "standard English" came from the parents themselves. Sometimes when he paid me, I'd comment on the learning materials. The illustrations were of white children braving weather conditions that would never occur near the equator. We branded a mistake any usage that might hint a Hongkonger was from Hong Kong.

As I said things like that, Benny tapped his phone. He hit each letter slowly, considering himself the sort of person who was above pretending to type while someone was talking, but quite happy to stretch out the composition of a real message until they'd finished. Sometimes his baseball cap said Nike, and sometimes Disneyland Paris.

Finally, Benny pronounced. "Is it racist," he said, "when my Connemara company sells seaweed to the Irish?"

The question did not wholly illuminate matters for me.

"The parents are paying," Benny said. He started typing again.

On my lunch break I messaged Julian. Unusually, he sent a long reply. He said Benny possibly meant—big "possibly," but possibly—that it was white-saviorish to think Hongkongers didn't know their own interests in a world where, like it or not, children got ahead with "standard" English. Parents couldn't change society, so they aimed for its inequalities to harm someone else's child rather than their own. Julian's mother had made that choice when she sent him to public school, and mine had when she'd told me not to say "amn't."

He often surprised me by coming out with statements like that. Something I admired in him was that he could calmly note where he benefited from unfairness—not self-indulgently like I often did, but factually.

I wondered if he'd always been that way. From my social media due diligence, I'd discovered that at Oxford he'd written poetry. There was a picture of him rowing for Balliol, which made me certain he wouldn't have gone near me aged twenty and had only started liking weird girls as a consequence of his boring job. For a while I luxuriated in thinking they'd all been normal but me, I was the only strange person who'd ever fascinated him so, and I alone stroked every contour of his mind. Then I found his girlfriend from final year, saw her doing spoken word at an open mic with her black cropped turtleneck and taut stomach complete of fucking course with navel piercing, and hated everything.

I deliberated whether he saw renouncing verse and boats as a success or a failure, but knew if I asked, he'd say some Julian thing about how he didn't waste time having thoughts on his life.

———

"Am I interesting?" I said one Saturday night. We'd just come back from seeing his friends.

"Potentially," he said. "You're a deadbeat. Some people find that interesting."

"Do you?"

"No."

"Then why do you like me?"

"Who said I liked you?"

Scatty raindrops tapped against the window like birds' feet. The dark shaded him: he could be someone else and I'd never know, which meant I could be anyone, too. And he always did take my side. Or approved when I took his, which was nearly as good. I wondered if I could kiss him and be sarcastic about it, but felt the humor wouldn't travel.

"Has knowing me made things different for you?" I said.

"Different how?"

"Do you feel different on the inside?"

"I suppose it's a comfort having you."

"How soon did you realize you were into me?" I said.

"Aesthetically, right away," he said. "If that's what you're asking."

"I couldn't tell if you liked me for ages."

"How about you?"

"When did I realize?" I said. "Right away. Aesthetically."

I sensed potential here for similar shots to our backhand over dreamy Seb. With a few words we could each come to think that the person beside us had jumped every time their phone buzzed, and that we ourselves had eventually got around to letting them have us. Neither of us lost anything by letting the other have that in their head. We both got a great deal out of having it in ours. It was almost collaboration, which was close enough to partnership. But I was tired.

"The first time I saw you," I said, "I thought you'd know where to get everything cheaper."

"That's a terrible impression of me."

"I know. This was back when I thought bankers were good with money."

"Savage. Fair."

"But I didn't put much thought in. When I met you."

"I can't say it was an epoch in my life either. I was curious. I realized the curiosity would probably survive the encounter, so then I asked you to lunch."

I wanted him to say more.

Because I loved him—potentially. That, or I wanted to be him, or liked being someone to whom he assigned tasks. I'd had no livable spaces in Hong Kong until I met him, so possibly I just loved thinking in silence and breathing clean air—if that was a tenable distinction when I did so in his apartment.

"Julian," I said, "what are we?"

"Fucked if I know."

"Fucked anyway."

"Your zest for life is infectious."

"Just as well you're immune."

We were doing what he and Miles did—acting out scenes. He did that with everyone: extemporized until he'd decided his dynamic with them, then held on to it for dear life.

"Do you love me?" I said.

What he said next didn't hurt me. It was exactly what I'd been looking for to murder the outgrowth.

"I like you a great deal," he said. "Now go to sleep."

16

I saw now that I had a persistent and stupid fantasy where Julian said he loved me. He wouldn't expect to hear it back. He'd just need to say it, and would be fully contented once he had. This was unfair to ask of him, did not cohere with what I claimed to want from him, and was not something he was at all likely to do. Anyway, he'd said it had ended with Kat in part because she was pushy about things like "I love you." I, however, was reasonable.

I'd noticed Julian used the passive with an unidentified subject whenever he talked about their breakup—"It ended with Kat"—which was poor form stylistically.

———

The week after Julian's birthday, one of his Oxford friends threw a soirée at their split-level open-plan eco-friendly flat. The more compound adjectives describing an apartment, the higher the rent. Julian put me on the big leather couch and left to mingle without me. He didn't consciously plan this series of actions, but I hardly knew anyone, so that was the effect.

His dreamy lawyer friend Seb came and sat with me. Seb's tie was undone and still on his neck, as though he'd fought to leave a meeting but they'd need him back any minute now. His hair was ruffled, giving the troublingly simultaneous impression that he'd also just had sex. While he talked, I remembered the "dreamy Seb" exchange and had to remind myself Seb wasn't in on the joke.

I asked about work. "Busy," Seb said. Then I asked how he'd joined his firm. He said he'd finished uni not knowing what to do and thought law would keep him happy and solvent.

"Has it?" I said.

"It's kept me solvent."

Seb's composure and Julian's were quite different. Julian's came from an equanimous trust that most things were quite beneath his notice. Seb had a more active bearing. Every sentence seemed a decision.

As he talked, I started planning what it would be like to have sex with him. That was what I called it, "planning," when I pondered how I'd fuck someone I had no current intention of fucking. One had to be prepared, I felt. For Seb, I'd spend a great deal of time with my hand near his belt buckle and see if he nudged me down to touch him or up to undo it. Julian sometimes did one and sometimes the other, so never let anyone tell you men are not complex.

Seb kept topping up my glass. I said I was fine, really.

"Afraid you'll end up with a red face?" he said. "It's hereditary. Happens to all the Irish anyway. One more."

Julian's chinless wonders often started attractive, then lapsed the more they said.

A man in an idiotic shirt asked Seb to come and tell them about the time he'd scaled the wall at Magdalen when the porters locked the doors. Julian came back over to me when he'd left, which made me smile. He must have been watching us. I hoped he'd kiss me, or at least take my arm, but I knew him better than that. He didn't "mark his turf," would sooner die than use that phrase without scare quotes, would explain his non-turf-demarcation with reference to feminism, and felt in addition but less vocally that he was above such Neanderthal theatrics.

So he took my glass off me, gave me a tissue—to intimate I'd smudged my lipstick—and glanced in Seb's direction. "Jane wouldn't like it," he said. And that was that.

"How together are they?" I said.

"Very," Julian said.

"What about you?" I said. "Would you mind?"

He looked at me with a mix of concern and derision, like I'd just asked what country we were in.

"Don't take coke off him," he said.

Numbers dwindled. I went upstairs to the bathroom and topped up my makeup, staring at my face until it seemed like someone else's. Jane "wouldn't like it," and that made me happy. I'd only met Jane once, but she seemed like another Victoria: it was as if someone else ironed everything for her—her whole life—and her role was to make new creases.

When I came out, a dozen guests were left on the open floor downstairs. I was about to join them when I heard deep voices from the balcony in front: Julian, Seb, Ralph.

"Where's Galway Girl?" Seb said.

Julian said he didn't know.

They stood facing away from me at the railing ahead, looking down on the rest of the party. I tiptoed back and stood flat against the wall.

The playlist downstairs shuffled to Duke Ellington—"Blood Count."

"The accent," Seb said. "Like a gypo with elocution lessons."

Ralph laughed. Julian didn't. From the atrium the trumpets dithered like jurors. When the silence became obvious, Ralph looked between the others, who stood still.

Finally, Julian said: "I think you've had enough, mate, if you're slurring the wrong ethnicity."

Seb nudged Ralph. "If you'd seen her when I said the Irish have red faces."

Julian reached into his pocket, then seemed to remember he

couldn't smoke indoors. Seb surveyed the party. Ralph took an interest in his watch.

Then Julian said: "Would you like a crack at the Polish while we're here?"

"My mum's Polish," Seb said.

"Really?" Julian said.

"And she voted Leave."

"Right."

"Plenty of Poles did."

"Right."

"And Irish," Seb said.

"Your mum's Irish, too?"

"The Irish voted Leave. My mum's Polish."

"How on earth did the Irish vote Leave?"

Ralph coughed. "Seb's mum can't be Polish," he said, "or Julian would have got to her by now."

No doubt in Ralph's head he had shrewdly split his fealties by alleging that Julian had sex with people who weren't British, and that Seb's mother had sex with anyone. His compatriots appeared not to see it that way.

"Look," Seb said, "leave Agnieszka out of this."

"Words cannot express how happy I am to leave Agnieszka out of this," Julian said.

"I just think it's specious."

"What's specious?"

"Fucking an Irish girl and then saying I can't hold my drink."

Julian nodded, then said with some gravity: "I do see the hypocrisies."

"Beggin' yer pardon for any offense," Seb said, "but you can tell she grew up in a small house."

Julian straightened up. So did Seb.

"How can you tell?" Ralph said.

"I reckon Julian's more of an authority," Seb said. "On the subject."

"What subject?"

"The subject of girls from small houses."

Silence.

Ralph said: "What do they say?"

Seb said: "About girls from small houses?"

"Yeah."

Seb paused for timing.

Then: "Small house, cavernous throat."

Ralph laughed. The sax stewed magisterially. Julian said nothing.

Then Seb inclined his head as if moving things along. "I do see the appeal," he said, "given you're not actually with her."

Glasses clinked downstairs. The drums banged like gavels.

Julian said nothing.

Julian changed the subject.

17

In the middle of February, Julian said he'd be in London for a few months. I wanted to ask what "a few" meant, but decided not to give him the satisfaction.

We were at Central Pier. I wore a trench coat with the belt tied in a bow. He debriefed me on logistics with his hand on my waist, and I thought: gift-wrapped.

Then I looked out on the water, thinking: stocks float, but I wonder if bankers do. It was the first time I'd explicitly imagined his death and I wondered if he'd envisaged mine or if he was as withholding on this point as he was about I love you. I didn't want him to fantasize about killing me—unless I did—but him finding me in a lake could be really quite affecting. Not all women idly contemplated whether their partners wanted to murder them and whether the prospect appealed, and if they did it was society that was sick, not them.

"Shall we head?" he said.

I smiled and thanked him for letting me stay in his absence. When we got home, I went to my room and cried.

The next day at work, I taught my eleven-year-olds how to write letters of complaint. No contractions, I said. They were excited to start airing grievances.

"We'll stay in touch, of course," he'd said.

Letters of complaint said what you wanted done and the deadline for doing it. Eleven-year-olds would never write them. They were nice people. But they had to in exams. We didn't test whether they could ask their boss for enough money to survive—but if the barista forgot their macchiato, they needed top-notch English ready to fire.

At home that evening, I told Julian about this. I asked why we taught kids to see themselves as customers when in fact they would spend a greater share of their living hours producing things than buying them.

"Ask Miles," he said. "You guys can touch base while I'm away."

Real people, I said, did not "touch base." They talked.

"Do that, then," he said. "Talk."

My banker friend Julian said more things then. I thought of the water.

PART II

EDITH

18

MARCH

Edith Zhang Mei Ling—English name Edith, Chinese name Mei Ling, family name Zhang—was a Hong Kong local, but she'd gone to boarding school in England, then to Cambridge. She was twenty-two like me, and now worked at Victoria's law firm. Her accent was churchy, high-up, with all the cathedral drops of English intonation. Button, water, Tuesday—anything with two syllables zipped up then down like a Gothic steeple. Three-syllable words spread out like the spokes on an umbrella: "attaches" became "a-tach-iss." She said "completely" a lot and usually dropped the "t" in the middle. Besides school and uni, she hadn't seen much of the UK.

"You should see Dublin," I said.

I saw her begin to say Dublin wasn't in the UK, remember I knew, too, and wonder why I'd said that. I wondered, too. She'd be a sight walking down my road: perfect posture, knee-high slouched boots, glossy tong-curled hair, small black handbag on a silver chain. Dad and George would regard her like a viscountess's cougar they'd been paid to petsit without knowing whether it had teeth.

Her manicure was perfect, though I noted with interest that she kept her nails short.

It was the beginning of March. We queued for a play at the

Academy for Performing Arts, a tall concrete building on Gloucester
Road. Someone at Edith's firm had spare tickets. Edith asked Victoria, who couldn't make it and so passed the invite on to me. It took
bullet-biting to accept it, but I googled Edith, and her profile picture—
drinking coffee in Ubud, hair Gallically bunned—convinced me to go.
Her Instagram had highlights pinned from European trips. From this
I speculated that she'd picked up her hair knots and her morning cap-
puccino abroad, though this was probably too crass to be something
she'd really do. She was too sophisticated for me to reverse-engineer
how she'd got there.

Besides, Julian had been gone two weeks now, and I wanted to feel
like a person again.

"How are you liking Hong Kong?" Edith said, as though I'd moved
last week.

"It's great," I said.

"You don't seem like most TEFL teachers."

That shouldn't have made me happy, but it did.

She was a few inches shorter than me, but side by side our waists
were level, which meant she had proportionally longer legs. It felt re-
laxing to compare our bodies. It wasn't the fretful ranked surveyal of
my teens so much as a hazy curiosity.

She had fun-size cartons of soya milk in her bag and offered me
one while she talked on the phone. "Hou ah, hou ah, mou man tai,"
she said. "M goi sai."

The play was a Chekhov number in Russian, with Chinese and
English surtitles. We were too near the front to see both the words
and the actors' faces at once, so we had to choose which to follow.
Throughout, Edith tended to her work inbox. She managed this by
holding her bag like a lapdog and thumbing away inside it. I wondered
if the actors noticed.

One man wore a monocle. Another carried perfume and intermit-
tently doused himself. You knew the women by their dresses: white
for ingenue, navy for spinster, black for wife. There was vodka and,

presumably, adultery. I decided to read the surtitles so I could fill Edith in later, but it was all a tangle of Olgas and Mashas and catalyzed interpersonal tension.

A man lost a duel. Edith started at the gunshot. Curtain call.

"Did you like it?" she said as we left.

"As much as I could follow," I said.

"Well, I thought it was exceptional. Shall we do it again sometime?"

I tried to hide my excitement.

***

Edith had come into my life just when there was a vacancy.

Julian had been in London a few weeks now. He sent messages. I never read them right away. First, like a stress test, I'd list the worst things he could say. Things like: I'm back with Kat and we're getting married. Our relationship was an elaborate social experiment which has now exhausted my interest. I'm subletting the apartment and you need to leave. I'm not subletting but you still need to leave.

Once I'd modeled out every possible way the message could hurt me, I went somewhere quiet and opened it. Then it didn't say anything I'd worried about and I felt I'd got away with something, but that I'd be found out next time.

In person, if I missed a shaking hand or a falter in his smile, then that was that and I couldn't revisit it. But in written form he was under a bell jar and would stay there until my analyses were complete. Of course he had me under one as well, but I chose my phrasing carefully and knew it would stand up to scrutiny. Really it was a shame we had bodies. I wrote: i miss having sex with you but only because i have a body, & if i didn't then everything would be easier. He replied that on the contrary, he suspected sex without bodies might pose challenges.

Sunday mornings were Saturday for him. His papers came as usual. I laid them on the coffee table, read the headlines, and fidgeted with my watch. He'd left some shirts behind that I still hadn't ironed.

The creases seemed like his, though I knew they were the washing machine's. I watched movies in his bed. This was in theory no different to doing so in my own, but I found it more immersive.

Sometimes he rang on the weekend, but more often he messaged. Like me, he seemed to find it easier to express himself behind a screen. The Saturday after my theater date with Edith, he wrote:

> Feel we may have parted on bad terms. Suboptimal terms certainly. Hope you're keeping up with Miles, Victoria, Ralph-pronounced-Rafe, etc. It's mental here. The garçon absolut still too principled to want to win elections, which is splendid now Tories have called one. & Bank of England says we're not doing enough to prepare for no deal—so between May grabbing Damocles by the sword & the rest of us stocking up on canned beans, London is, as ever, a haven of quietude. Interesting how pitch has changed from "Take back control" to "We think there will still be food." Anyway. Say if you need anything. Sorry for uncertainty re: when back. J.

An editor could have fun, I thought, going through his messages and changing the full stops to exclamation marks.

I didn't tell him about my evening with Edith. I couldn't be bothering him with every tiny detail.

A fortnight after we met, Edith had theater tickets again. This time she asked me first, and then the next week, too. I didn't tell Victoria. I hoped the longer I left it, the more dudgeon it would cause her. I liked dudgeoning Victoria. And it was private, all of it—listening to the pinnacles and spires of her accent, sizing our proportions, feeling with each play like I was more and more someone Edith would be friends with.

After the first play, I'd googled her boarding school tuition and the international student fees at Cambridge. I was unsurprised when she said her parents worked in finance. In the interval of the second play, I said something in passing about posh English people, and Edith said the concept of poshness didn't exist in Hong Kong. It was like Ireland: all money was new money. Rich was posh and posh was rich. Given that I was neither, I wasn't sure why I found that comforting, but I did. There wasn't even an upper-class accent, Edith said, although mainland Cantonese was regarded by "some" as sounding nicer.

On each outing she spouted facts at me. She used her hands when she talked, and often her whole body. To show me the regions of China, she scribbled on a napkin. I kept it. I liked her enthusiasm. I couldn't remember the last time I'd met someone who got excited about things.

Each play she had a different handbag. She managed this by putting the same abundantly pocketed travel case inside them all, so that the outer bag on any given day was just a shell. The designer bags cost thousands of Hong Kong dollars, and the travel case was maybe a hundred, and the latter was where she actually kept her things. I'd never understand rich people. Edith's keys, Octopus card, and wallet all "lived" in a given crevice, so that she could quickly locate them. This I admired and tried to implement in my own life. But I would choose bad places for things to "live," forget they lived there, and still not be able to find them.

When I closed shop with Joan before seeing the third play, she asked what I was up to. I said: off to the theater. Joan's face said: I'm clearly paying you too much, and Joan's mouth said: enjoy.

——

My days off were Sunday and Monday. In the staffroom I complained with everyone else that working on Saturdays was killing my social life, but I didn't have one. That was fine. I liked having space to think. Besides, the rush-hour train served for company. I settled in under a man's armpit, felt the stud of a woman's handbag digging into me, and thought: I am a part of something.

Weekends were harder. The flat was louder without Julian. The taps dripped like waterboards, and the neighbors argued next door. Some mornings I didn't leave the bed because then I'd have to brush my teeth, followed by a series of actions that amounted to living my life as the person I was. I was unable to drum up positivity about either dental hygiene or the rest of my day, so I told myself I was disgusting and lazy and I'd be late and they'd fire me, and then I got up. If you were really sick you couldn't just harness your self-loathing like that, so I knew I was fine. And Edith was becoming something to look forward to.

19

The Sunday after my third theater date with Edith, I went to see Miles at his flat in Kennedy Town. Julian had asked me to. I suspected he wanted to make sure I was getting out of the flat, since he'd never gone much himself. But it would have been childish to tell him I knew what he was up to.

The main room in Miles's flat was painted mustard and stuffed with clashing furniture. For an academic's home, there weren't many books. I guessed from the Kindle on the table that he was moving with the times.

We talked about his university, and then how it compared to where I'd gone. Miles said Julian had told him I'd got a "very good first indeed," and asked if I'd thought about academia.

"It seems interesting," I said, "but I don't know what I'd write about."

I couldn't tell if Miles was quoting or paraphrasing the "very-indeed" construction. Julian sometimes went sarcastically anti-quated, which showed he meant what he was saying or he wouldn't bother sounding like he didn't. Miles, though, might say "very-indeed" quite naturally. My degree was a fact, being a number, and Julian's opinion couldn't change its value. But I often thought about things that were silly to think about.

"Is your book going well?" I said.

"No," Miles said, "but it's never going well."

He asked if sudoku interested me and said he had a book of puzzles if it did. We played in silence. Soon I got bored and sharpened his pencils. He kept them in a box on the table.

"You're a gem," he said. "Julian's done well for himself."

It was the most explicitly Miles had ever alluded to the relationship. I felt shortchanged that my lead-whittling abilities had triggered this acknowledgment.

Then I wondered if I'd really just come to add texture to dinner with Florence—to see if Miles mentioned anything about her taste in decor, for instance. This seemed depressing if true. If I was stockpiling curlicues for Florence evenings while doing nothing to improve my real situation, it would mean I cared more about my interior life than the tangible one. Julian didn't daydream, and thus was off in London with a real job while I was a TEFL waster—though he read so much that maybe he did have an imagination and was just better at controlling it. I'd never know if other people were as graphic as me in their daydreams and we all just pretended we weren't. I'd once googled "what do serial killers think about." There was surprisingly little overlap, but I hid my thoughts anyway. The more I imagined things, the more personal they felt.

"It can be challenging making friends when you've first moved here," Miles said, snapping me out of it. "A lot of my exchange students find it quite isolating."

"I have one or two," I said. I thought: one here, one there. The word "friend" did Herculean work in terms of describing me and Julian. And now I had another friend.

———

A new class of ten-year-olds started on Tuesday. To break the ice, I asked why they wanted to learn English. They looked at each other across a room so small they could barely pull out the chairs, and seemed unsure that the premise held.

Lydia Tam introduced herself, then said, "My Chinese name is—" before another girl dug her in the ribs and said she couldn't give it here. Their motives for studying English were, from most to least commonly cited: school, travel, to watch movies, and to talk to me. This last was from Denise Chan, a lick-arse, but you couldn't call your students that.

Next came Fergus Wong, who wanted to learn English because everything had an English name as well as a Cantonese one.

"You're crazy," said Denise. This seemed to be what Hongkongese ten-year-olds said to someone when they didn't understand what they meant.

I hated wielding authority. The kids could tell that, and responded poorly whenever I tried. So I let them talk, and thought: Edith Zhang, Zhang Mei Ling, Edith Zhang Mei Ling. I said the words to myself like I was unwrapping something.

20

APRIL

When Julian had been gone just over a month, Edith and I went to Cinema City JP on Paterson Street. The movie was dubbed badly in Cantonese. We knew what would happen before the opening credits. Edith liked that: formulaic plots were easier to follow while she edited documents on her iPad. We sat away from everyone else, the film started, and her keyboard clacked like chattering teeth. She didn't tell me how much her firm paid her, but I guessed it was a lot.

The following week we went for coffee in Sheung Wan. In the queue, Edith told me she liked how I'd done my hair. I was momentarily happy, but then she complimented the barista in the same animated way.

"Tell me about your family," she said at the table, as if fascinated that I had one.

I did. In return, she told me her father was from Hunan province in mainland China. Her mum was Singaporean. She only considered herself Hongkie in that she'd grown up there, and even then, she was born abroad. Her mum had nipped over to Toronto to get Edith a Canadian passport, a trek Mrs. Zhang regularly invoked for maternal leverage. She'd remind Edith that she flew while so pregnant she could barely walk and without Edith's father there, all to get her daughter a document that would make it easier to one day leave her.

In Mr. Zhang's defense, he had planned to be present at Edith's birth but had missed his flight. Mrs. Zhang almost named Edith "Toronto" to commemorate the affair. Mr. Zhang convinced her it was gauche. The only way Mr. Zhang could turn Mrs. Zhang's mind against a given course of action was by convincing her it was gauche.

"If I'm making my family sound really quite something," Edith said, "that's because they're really quite something."

We'd known each other four weeks at that point, but it felt like longer.

She said she fancied a pastry and queued up to get one. I watched her from the table. Edith disliked waiting but liked the order of queues. I saw from her tactfully impatient expression that she was doing her best to reconcile these stances. She was such a polished and resolute individual that tiny breaches stood out: stray thread on skirt, wisps where hairline met back of neck. Before I met her I'd wondered if "uncouth" meant uncouth then what did "couth" mean, and now I knew: "couth" meant Edith. That day, I realized I didn't care what anyone else thought. We could be thrown out of the café and I would think it just showed that they did not recognize genius.

Alone in bed that night I googled her. She was a trainee solicitor and her headshot was on the firm's website. There was a video underneath where she told prospective applicants that if she had to pick one thing, just one thing, that she loved most about work, it had to be the people. Her hair was in loose curls that bounced when she moved her chin. She nodded out her enthusiasms: the culture, nod, the ignition, nod, the fettle, nod, the élan. Such was corporate law.

I envied her conviction, and wondered if this was because I wanted to feel better about my own job.

Then I checked my phone: she'd just followed me on Instagram. When you followed someone first, you knew they would click on your name to see if they should follow back. And of course I saw her pictures

when I did that. I wasn't strictly obliged to keep scrolling and flick to
the ones she was tagged in, but it was expected behavior.

———

The next day, Victoria mined me about Julian in a French tearoom
with striped upholstery. She thumbed the quilting of her Chanel bag,
the squares threaded in penitential lines, and she dug. Questions. I'd
known she wanted him since she told me when drunk, but I couldn't
gauge if her sober self realized how transparent she was being.

More curious still: I played along. I wanted nuggets about Edith,
and Victoria gave me them.

"How have you been, Ava?" Victoria said, stressing the auxiliary so
I'd know she didn't care.

"Fantastic," I said, hitting the middle syllable to remind her I was
thriving specifically in Julian's apartment. "It's been so long"—vowels
elongated to clarify, in case I'd been too subtle, that I lived there and
she didn't.

"Your hair looks lovely," Victoria said—I should cut it. "Have you
cut it?"—Victoria saloned monthly, but kindly remembered to ask as
though for me it was a triennial treat, when to her it was a basic living
expense—conveying the latter, too, though, since we had to be honest
about these things.

Women are good at talking.

Menu, linen paper. The teas were in French, English, and Chinese,
in that order. Victoria ordered thé au citron. Her slight mispronuncia-
tion of "citron" presented a quandary. I could order it, too, and say it
properly. I wouldn't if she'd really butchered it, since that would be
crass—but a slight difference would prickle her without letting her
feel cathartically wronged. Alternatively, I could ask for lemon tea
and make her feel gaudy for having used French in the first place. I
would read out the English, then meet her eye: my niveau de français
is between me and God.

I could also just order a different tea, as I'd planned to before she said "thé au citron" wrong, but that was no fun.

"The lemon tea," I said. Then, waiting long enough that it was plausible the waiter was confused, but not so long he'd obviously already understood: "—sorry, the thé au citron."

Men weren't all I could do.

The waiter brought our tea with a military step. Victoria asked when Julian was back. I said I didn't know. Normally I wouldn't have admitted that—I would have implied I knew but was only authorized to share it with our very closest friends—but I wanted it settled so we could get to Edith.

From this implied level of communication with Julian, Victoria could gather I also didn't know if he was sleeping with other people in London, or indeed in Hong Kong. Whether Julian had multiple women on the go was in any case too ambiguous for her purposes. If he didn't, that might indicate he was—of all things to picture him saying—a one-woman man. If he did, his bandwidth might be full, between the side hustles and the regular Irish. Gobbets about Julian without clear implications did not interest Victoria. She was businesslike in this. If she could have offered him money to have sex with her, I knew she would. Equally, she wouldn't go near him if he accepted.

Next, Edith. She and Victoria were only acquaintances. No boyfriend, to Victoria's knowledge. Back in Hong Kong from England a little over a year, just finished the PCLL, now on her training contract. Victoria was an associate. (I hadn't asked Victoria if she outranked Edith, but Victoria thought I ought to know.) Most of Edith's friends were from boarding school, Cambridge, and law, and so, functionally, had money. (Victoria didn't clarify "functionally," since it was unimportant to Victoria whether someone cultivated a circle of rich people or just found themselves in one, but I supplied it myself.)

None of this was news, but I still liked hearing it.

It was obvious why Victoria wanted to know about Julian and

much less apparent why I was grilling her on Edith. Victoria, too, would be puzzled if she considered it—but she had a pit viper's brain. She saw not by looking but by rendering images of prey. She noticed all of Julian and the parts of me that pertained to him, and the rest she ignored.

If interested in Victoria, Julian would undoubtedly have some take about monogamy being contractual and the cheating element therefore being her and Ralph's problem. Going on precedent, Julian showed attraction by purchasing gifts and being inadvertently rude about your background, neither of which I'd seen him do to her. Anyway, I hated her, felt ill picturing them together, and told myself my information made no difference so I could trade it for facts about Edith.

We split the bill.

―――

English has a subjunctive. I learned that fact the morning I taught it. I knew French had one and suspected Irish did, but hadn't noticed its moody fingerprints on my native language.

It turned out I didn't know because the English subjunctive required phrasing I would never use. Apparently, you didn't say: "What if I was attracted to her." You said: "What if I were."

You deployed the subjunctive for the less-than-factual. If I avoided it, did that mean I only said true things? Or since I didn't section off the imaginary, perhaps everything I said was just a wish or a feeling. And maybe I sounded stupid for not knowing grammar. I wondered if Edith had been fighting the urge to correct me.

"What's the difference?" asked Kenny Chan.

I wasn't confident of it myself, so I read slowly from the textbook, then rephrased until they pretended to understand. But Sybil Fu got all the exercises right. She wouldn't have a few months ago. I knew it had nothing to do with me and everything to do with the fact that her parents literally paid her for getting good results, but it still made me happy.

I'd discovered that as well as her main Instagram account, Edith had one for her art. There were no references to it on the one she'd followed me from, but her friend Heidi had tagged it in a post she'd made a year ago. (Heidi had gone to boarding school with Edith, which was a normal thing for me to know because Edith had mentioned this in a comment that had come up on my newsfeed. My clicking Heidi's name and going through her posts was less obviously the algorithm's fault.)

On the art account Edith posted pencil sketches of buildings. Her scratchy, crosshatched style surprised me, but you could tell it was her from the odd careful detail. She was good. This came as some relief. I'd found the journals Julian had written poetry for at Oxford but hadn't dug further because I was worried the poems would be bad and I'd have to keep living in his apartment.

Edith's personal account was also an aesthetic triumph. The images were cool-toned and slightly faded, just enough to give reality a glaze. Her posts were like clues: here is some Edith, and some more over here, and an entire Edith somewhere beyond the squares. The things in the pictures obsessed me—the vintage gold-plate watch, the brown Saffiano iPhone folio case, the jade bracelet.

I wanted her life. I worried this might endanger our friendship, but so far it seemed to be facilitating it. Because she was richer and more important than me, I had an out from the suspicion that I was in fact her lesser on intellectual or moral grounds. She answered her phone or tapped at something on her iPad, and I thought: everyone else wants a piece of her, and here she is with me. This was stupid because when Julian had done that, I'd just resented him for not paying me attention—and I'd known him far longer than a month. Probably I was a bad person and could not correctly process emotions.

My collarbone was a comfort. I could find myself otherwise grotesque and still trace the lines in front of the mirror, thinking: this is sexy. This I would fancy if I were Edith and if I, Edith, liked women.

E dith and I were now hanging out a few times a week, but I had no idea why she spent time with me, let alone why she liked me. I supposed I was of anthropological interest. She'd ask why I didn't "just" do things. Why, she'd say, didn't I "just" check the weather before leaving the house, or "just" use an app for this or that—and she found it fascinating when I said I hadn't thought of it. Nothing escaped her. At a brunch place she referenced my not liking cheese, and when I asked how she knew that, she said I'd told her a few weeks ago. I never admitted to remembering things people had told me in passing. But I knew that this trait, which made Edith look frank and organized, would only make me seem like I didn't get out enough.

"You need to read the news," she said over coffee. "We can't even choose our own candidates, and I read the news."

I wanted to tell her I'd known that about Hong Kong's government, then remembered I only knew it because Julian had mentioned it the first time we met Miles.

I tried to see myself as she did when I dressed myself or bought things. The day before a cinema trip, I spent 400 Hong Kong dollars on a Jo Malone candle because I could imagine lighting it with her in the flat. For her, I'd burn a candle worth four hours' pay to me, i.e.

one-sixth of a day, thinking: the other five-sixths are there, too, if you want them. It would glow purple against her face and her cheekbones would ridge like sand ripples. She'd say I had good taste, and I'd say: no, you. We'd both be right because no one with discernment could spend that much time with another who lacked it. We both had it or neither did. And I didn't care which.

This made me realize I didn't actually care about refinement and just wanted Edith to like me. At first that made me happy, since earning her approval seemed more attainable than developing style. Then I remembered that Edith was not like most people.

I noticed more and more how much attention she paid to details. We went back again for lattes in Sheung Wan and she flinched when I sipped mine before she had taken a photo. Then she reconsidered the still life before her, and said: "Actually, the lipstick stain is perfect." I hadn't noticed I'd left one. Another day we got croissants and she said something in Cantonese, then translated—"Camera eats first"—as I made to pick mine up. That made me smile. I liked when she was unapologetically earnest about things, even if it was the angle of a pastry. She said Instagram made her look at everything more closely. Whenever she felt sad, she had a wall of happy memories to look back on.

"I know it's all very silly," she said, "but it's fun."

I tried to imagine Julian admitting he enjoyed something frivolous, and couldn't.

Besides, she wouldn't have said that the first month we met. I felt I was making progress, though I wasn't sure what towards. I wished I could watch her be friends with other women. If I knew how she normally went about it, it would be easier to know if we were different.

We laughed a lot in the cinema, especially at the films about sad straight boys who needed fixing. Women in movies taught men how to feel things. They took men who felt nothing and made them feel something. You could never tell what those women felt themselves, besides: I want to help this man. I'd never met anyone like that in real life.

I'd never met anyone like Edith either, and was grateful not to have many other people competing with her for my time. My Hong Kong existence was neat. It had space for her.

Besides, there was room in me. I felt superior to people like Scott and Madison, but really the three of us were hollow. They filled themselves with a little bit of everyone's approval, whereas I was more discerning. When I met someone I liked, I wanted all of them, and fast.

———

I started going to supermarkets a lot, mostly Wellcome and 7-Eleven trips. The walls were papered in adverts. The graying tiles bore boot marks and hairs set in mud. When I went at rush hour the cashier queues stretched down the aisles, and I'd take my place at the end and take things off shelves as I advanced. If you shuffled past your noodles or cereal or whatever, you couldn't go back or you'd lose your place in the line. I liked pretending this was the highest-risk transaction I participated in and that my life was well rooted aside from this one thing about the supermarket.

When Julian was around I'd committed to nutritionally sound shopping baskets. Now it was his second month away, I bought Pocky sticks and matcha KitKats. The packets listed ingredients I couldn't pronounce. I puzzled them out by breaking down the syllables like I made students do with names of dinosaurs.

On the weekends that I didn't see Edith or Miles, the convenience-store staff were the only people I spoke to. I made myself nice for them. I put on lipstick. At the counter an old lady with cropped hair turned to a colleague and said: gweimui ah. In Cantonese, white people were ghosts. In Hokkien, Edith had told me over coffee, we were redheads, and in Mandarin "old friends."

"The latter," she'd said, "is certainly one reading of Sino-Western relations."

In Russia, Edith had said, you could get Putin's face on anything.

Vodka, bread, you name it. In Hong Kong, the same was true of Hello Kitty. This was, Edith speculated, in part because Hello Kitty came from Japan and so betokened resistance to mainland China. A vending machine in her apartment lobby stocked Hello Kitty toy pianos and candy dispensers. There were also Hello Kitty tampons, though she was less certain what they stood for. I'd noticed she'd started talking more often about periods, also exfoliation and core-tightening exercises. I knew these were normal things for friends to discuss, but the thought came to me unbidden: maybe Edith wants me to notice her body.

One Sunday in mid-April, Victoria bumped into me leaving 7-Eleven and asked how I stayed thin if that was what I ate. "I strive for balance," I said, which meant I sometimes had a Hello Kitty doughnut for breakfast and then felt so sick I ate nothing else all day. "Balance," Victoria said, "is key." I agreed.

The following week she saw me there again. I recalled she lived nearby. We were both drunk. She asked what was wrong with me. I said nothing was wrong with me, that something was wrong with her, and also, while I was here and with reference to her previous query, that I was thin because I had money. The next time we saw each other, we pretended this exchange had not occurred.

I could say whatever I wanted now.

—

Edith was still always the one who suggested meeting up. I didn't dare. Her time, like Julian's, was important. I'd pretend I couldn't do the first day she proposed, but she'd say it was her only one free. If she posted no evidence of her hectic life, I thought: she said she was busy. When she did post I thought: not too busy for Instagram.

The other teachers invited me to TST. First we went to a speakeasy bar that was authentically local. Scott from Arkansas said he knew because another American had told him. There was no website or contact number, but Scott got us there by finding the 7-Eleven on

Kimberley Road and looking for the back door with a pig's head peeking out.

I went to the toilet. The girl in the next cubicle was crying or coming—I wasn't sure. Edith always posted stories on Friday nights. Sure enough, from 9 p.m. there was a pile of folders in the office captioned "My life is fun and interesting," followed an hour later by an overhead of cocktails with: "Liquor cures all workloads." I considered the possibility that the girl was both crying and coming, and felt her night was going better than mine regardless.

Too late I remembered that I'd have to post something now or Edith would see I'd viewed her story and think I was at home on my phone. I went back out and roped Briony from Leeds into a selfie. She'd taken too much MDMA to question this behavior. Twenty minutes later, I checked the list and saw Edith had seen it.

Soon enough, the rainbow circle appeared around Edith's name to show she'd put another picture up. I didn't check it. This felt like a minor victory.

The following Monday, we got coffee in Sheung Wan and Edith said she was working on an IPO—initial public offering, she clarified. I knew that from Julian but appreciated the thought. The partner helming it, William Brent, had been in Hong Kong since before the handover. He said men were scared of women now.

"I'm not sure," Edith said, "if he's scared he'll grope us or scared we'll tell HR."

She felt it had been easy at Cambridge to claim we should take unfeminist spaces and reform them. Harder in real life, she found. You couldn't quite announce to William Brent that the "space" of his law firm was presently unfeminist, not least because the first step to changing it would be expunging William Brent.

Edith was calm about things she couldn't change. Her firm was full of horrible men and she had to be nice to them. You did in every job, and at least hers paid well.

I was sure there were William Brents at Julian's bank, and that he took about as much action as he had when Seb commented on the dimensions of my throat. Undoubtedly he told himself he'd do something once he had the power—and when he got there, he'd wonder where all the women had gone.

I still hadn't told Edith about Julian. Probably I was putting it off because I knew she wouldn't like the sound of him. I wanted to say she didn't know him like I did. That was a textbook claim women made about men we'd regret—the men or the claim, depending on how you parsed it—but it was undeniably true when Edith and Julian had never met.

"You really don't like men," I said.

"You're right. I don't."

This, too, was ripe for parsing.

I told Edith about a summer in college when a few of us had gone to someone's holiday home in West Cork. I slept on the couch, two of the lads took a mattress on the floor, and in the dark one of them came and lay on top of me—calmly, as if instructed to. I whispered I wasn't sure, which meant get off but I'm scared what you'll do if I say that, and he ignored me. His breath tanged of alcohol. I thought it was Colm but it might have been Ferdia. I couldn't see. Probably I could have deduced Ferdia or Colm, but I didn't, because then I'd know, and then for all subsequent interactions with either Colm or Ferdia, which I'd have to keep having because no one would believe me or they'd say yeah but he's his own problems, I'd remember what he did, know his own memory of events was that we'd got drunk and hooked up, and be certain, too, that our friends would "not take sides," i.e. treat me like someone who might be lying about rape. I told myself what they'd say—gray area, I just don't think he'd do that—and soon became convinced I was actually making it up, then felt like a sick amoral person for falsely accusing someone of something that I hadn't accused him of and that he had in fact done.

"Fuck," said Edith.

"Yeah."

You could tell who'd been through it and who hadn't because when you told someone who hadn't, they were hungry for details. They'd say it was so they could experience their moral outrage with a loftier precision. They were liars and we hated them. Edith and I said as much as we wanted to. When we were done, we changed the subject.

One day I realized we'd stopped seeing plays. I asked why, and Edith said she didn't really like theater. "I wanted you to think I did," she said, and then went back to her phone. This surprised me on a few levels. I hadn't known she cared about making me think she was cultured. I hadn't realized I came across as someone who set store by that kind of thing. And I hadn't noticed our relationship changing such that she could now be honest with me—if this latest confession was what she really felt, and not some new illusion of candor.

Julian, I thought, can tell when people like him. He and Edith had many skills in common. I wondered if this was one of them.

———

I started drafting a message where I told Julian about Edith.

i've made a new friend. i don't know why i'm only telling you now. i've only known her a few weeks but i'm thinking about her more and more. incidentally, the search term "how to flirt with women" returns very different results to "how to tell a woman is flirting with you." in both cases the researcher is assumed to be male. i'm guessing you don't mind when things assume you're male, which might explain your love of literature.

i've never had sex with a woman anyway. i kissed a few in college. their lips are softer, if you didn't know.

i think about sleeping with other people and then i feel guilty, which is weird bc i think if anything you'd be amused if i didn't have sex with someone for your sake. like oh you shouldn't have it's too much. i was scared when you left but i don't think anything has changed. you still put more time and energy into showing you don't love me than anyone has ever put into showing me they do.

sometimes i love you and sometimes i think it would be best if a plane flew into your office and you were on the plane or in the building.

I decided, on balance, that this message would not have the propitiatory effect intended.

22

My Primary Four kids were writing haikus: five syllables, then seven, then five. The previous term they'd done four-line poems, and Ming Chuen Lai expressed a certain suspicion that this meant the curriculum was becoming easier, not harder. We argued over certain words. They held, for instance, that "film" had two syllables: "fill-um." I wanted to say most of Dublin agreed, but their parents weren't paying for Dublin English.

Katie Cheung, nine, disliked the haiku format. Together we brainstormed for her to write a poem about a cat. For the first line, she said: "The big hairy cat liked to drink lots and lots of milk."

I offered five-syllable versions: "My cat likes its milk," "The cat likes drinking," "Milk's my cat's favorite." (Whether "favorite" had two syllables or three was a box Pandora herself would have left well enough alone at that particular juncture.)

Katie Cheung wasn't assuaged. Katie Cheung wanted it all in the first line. I asked what she'd put in the second if she'd said everything in the first, and she said she'd think of more.

I told her she could write a story, but to at least use paragraphs. She acceded to this with great reluctance. There still wouldn't be room, she said.

I'd been a pliable child and I wondered if it was obvious, even then, that I would never be an artist. If a teacher had told me to put in line breaks, I'd have sliced up my words like ham in order to please them.

———

Mam told me Dublin was hot for April. "Next the Arctic will melt," she said. "And we'll be living in bunkers." I said I hoped there'd be intermediary stages.

She said Dad said hi. I said she meant Dad told her to say hi. "Dad says hi" implied he was saying it himself. Mam told me there was no need to be difficult, and that George said hi, too. Then she had news. My cousin Tadhg's landlady had evicted him, purportedly to move in a family member, but the room had gone on Daft a week later with a €100 hike in the rent. I'd forgotten about Tadhg. Another cousin had had a baby. I told Mam I didn't recognize the name, and she repeated: Sinéad, as though this alone would acquaint me with her. "You're far away," she said, which felt unfair inasmuch as I hadn't known Sinéad before I'd left either.

"Mam," I said, "did you think about giving us Irish names?"

She said no, that people who did that sent their kids to tin whistle classes.

"And Rachel Mulvey's back," she said. I didn't know Rachel Mulvey either. Mam specified: the Mulveys down the road, in a tone conveying: it is now obvious to me that my daughter knows nothing. "Back from New York," Mam said. "They all come back sooner or later." She added that the house felt empty without me and Tom. "It's a waste giving money to a landlord. Tom said eight hundred's a good deal. Eight hundred a month. For one room, Ava."

"It's wrong," I said, "when people earn money for owning houses they don't use. I think we should take their houses off them."

"Daydreaming again," Mam said.

Ringing home made me miss discussing politics openly. I couldn't at work, not least because Joan and Benny were both landlords on the side, but more fundamentally because bosses did not like to employ people who thought they should not exist. Julian listened but was incapable of going: that's an interesting thought. He'd swipe at anything dangled before him. With Edith and Miles I could be as left-wing as I wanted, but I worried about how to sound clever.

I said: "The state should seize all the hotels in Dublin and turn them into social housing."

"Ah now, Ava."

"And there should be a one hundred percent inheritance tax. And universal basic income."

"Ah now."

"And eventually communism."

"Ah now."

I enjoyed conversations where I wasn't attempting to persuade anyone, where I just said precisely what I thought. I got tired of making myself acceptable.

Mam started asking a lot of questions. She did that when she could tell I was holding something back. But there was nothing worth telling her about Edith. If I said I'd been getting coffee with a woman, Mam would just wonder what I was really hiding.

23

L ater in April, Edith and I went to an art exhibition in Sheung Wan. She greeted me with a hug. I was afraid I'd get something on her clothes—a piece of fluff or a stray hair.

"Nice dress," she said. "You look like Audrey Hepburn."

"It's old," I said.

"It's lovely."

She seemed to think I couldn't take compliments. I preferred to believe I disliked profuse displays of emotion, and would accept any amount of praise if people tempered themselves in how they expressed it.

On the walk over, I wondered if Edith was pretty or if I just found her so. I was aware, with my college head on me, that beauty was subjective—but I wanted to know if we were aesthetically matched. I nearly asked if she knew Holly Golightly was bisexual. Having formulated the remark and decided how I'd orchestrate my body language while making it, I blushed nearly as much as I would if I'd actually said it.

Lumpish children ran through the gallery. The paintings were of tulips and cherry blossoms. Edith claimed it was the kind of thing her grandma liked. I thought she'd said that to make fun of the exhibition, but then she went to buy prints for the very same grandma. It was at moments like this I remembered there was a category of people who called her Mei Ling and whom I'd never meet.

As we left, I told Edith I'd go home and make dinner. She asked if I had flatmates. I'd been wondering when she'd raise that.

"One," I said, "but he's away. Julian."

"Julian," she said—vigilantly, I thought. "Maybe we could cook together."

I'd never brought guests to the apartment and was relieved there was no tiresome process of registering them at the lobby. The rule was that you should, but it turned out to be one the doormen did not apply to white people. In the lift a woman held a panting German shepherd on a lead. Edith said something gao something, and the woman laughed and said something something gao.

"You're sure Julian doesn't mind?" Edith said.

I felt I had told her something personal by giving his name and wondered, stupidly, if it was too late to take it back.

Inside the door, I put my ballet flats on the bottom shelf, then moved them to the top unnecessarily, which struck me as the behavior of a nervous person. While Edith cooked, I lit the candles for the first time ever. I wondered if Julian would notice the globs of wax when he returned.

Edith took Julian's wingback chair after it became clear I'd forgotten I was meant to invite her to. She used the armrests. Julian rarely did when he sat there. He'd crossed his arms narrowly, like he was in the middle seat on a plane and the people on either side had boarded first.

We ate. I asked why Edith didn't move out. It would have been a stupid question for most Hongkongese twentysomethings, but I knew she made plenty of money.

"You can't just move out," she said. "You need a husband, or at least a mortgage."

"Do you think you'll get married?"

"No, I don't suppose I will."

"We should just get a house together."

Edith smiled and said: maybe.

I gave her the remote and she chose a channel showing *Inglourious Basterds*. She said the title was spelled that way because Tarantino had misspelled it in a leaked screenplay and then insisted he'd done it on purpose. We agreed this was extremely male.

I touched my mouth a lot when we talked. It was a childish habit and made me look gormless. I made myself stop, then found I was playing with my hair.

During a shootout, Edith asked what Julian was like. It did not seem strictly necessary for her to keep using his name.

"He's in London right now," I said. "He's in banking."

I considered alternative phrasings: he does banking, he works in a bank, he works for a bank. Edith probably thought they were all the same, but maybe she didn't and I'd used the wrong one. I sometimes thought things might have gone better with Julian if I'd known you went "up" to Oxford. I hated the British class system. That was definitely a front for whatever the hell I was actually feeling in the context of Edith, but it was also a real emotion—just not the main one. By my standards, I was being self-aware. I knew Julian still wouldn't be my boyfriend if I'd said "up," but on some level I earnestly believed that my key uncertainty with Edith was whether she experienced attraction towards people who misused the subjunctive.

"Do your parents find it weird?" Edith said. "That you're living with a man."

"I haven't told them. They wouldn't get it."

Which was true.

"Does he bring girls back?" she said. She was typing on her phone while she said it. I knew she really did have emails to answer, but I also wondered if it wasn't a touch convenient that she always saw to them when she was saying something potentially awkward.

I wished I'd said at the start that Julian and I were fucking. It was too late now. Edith would stop telling me things and would be newly suspicious of anything I told her.

Looking at her, I could see she'd suit Julian. They both kept tempo to hard shoes on marble floors, Sunday phone calls, and midnight emails. They could save time if one read the *Economist* and the other the *FT* and they then pooled facts. I was sure if I put all this on a spreadsheet, Julian would ask Edith out. I pictured them together, then realized I was only doing so because I couldn't form a clear image of her and me. My hand could pass as Edith's much more easily than as Julian's in the dark—but there were only so many thoughts you could productively entertain.

The film ended and Edith said she'd have to go soon. "We should do this again sometime," she said.

"It might be harder when Julian's back."

"He's not a mingler?"

I said he was about as close to being Catherine the Great of Russia. This joke was a lot like one of Julian's and wasn't much like mine. I wondered if I'd stolen his phraseology because it had worked on me.

Before Edith left, I showed her my wardrobe. She pulled out a camel coat and said she loved Ted Baker because it looked more expensive than it was. I had moved on so far from the version of myself who'd found the price alarming that I was only embarrassed on their behalf.

"By the way, Ava," she said, "are you a socialist?"

No one had asked me that before. At college people had assumed I was since all my friends were, and no one at work thought an adult could be. "Yes," I said. Edith said she saw the merits of it but also liked having nice things.

The next day I messaged saying: you could argue marxism means thinking everyone should have nice things, including us. Edith replied that I surely couldn't think it justified having a Rolex in the here and now, not when people were starving. I said: you're right. I wanted to add that Julian's watch was a cheap one he'd got in Shanghai, but reflected that Edith did not know him and had made no apparent horological assumptions.

Later that night, she messaged again, complaining about still being in the office. I sent her the PDF of *Why Marx Was Right* with the subject heading "warning: marxist polemic." She replied: are you hitting on me? because i feel like this won't be safe for work.

The lights were off. My hands were silhouettes in front of the screen.

———

Ever since his departure two months ago, I'd been keeping tabs on Julian online. His social media presence was more of an absence: no status updates, Facebook profilers changed so infrequently that within four scrolls he was getting sprayed with champagne after finals. He had an Instagram where he'd posted eight pictures ever. Since leaving for London, he'd taken to opening all my stories. I doubted he knew that it told you when someone did that.

Edith's name was always near the top of my story viewers. In vain I consulted articles and subreddits to see whether this meant she stalked me, I stalked her, or both. I already knew I checked her account a lot, but I wanted to know if the algorithm knew. More importantly, I wondered if I was high on Edith's list. If her coming high on mine did mean I was the stalker, then at least I would only come high on hers if she was stalking me, too—and if her being high on mine made her the stalker, then yes, my being high on hers would out me as one, but she stalked me back and couldn't judge.

I compared them. They were neither similar enough to be twins nor different enough to be foils. Still I kept one tab open on Edith, another on Julian, and went back and forth.

24

MAY

In early May, Edith took me to Times Square mall. It was big and clean, with marble floors. The Lane Crawford department store took up the atrium, then Gucci and Chanel ("tourist-bait," Edith said), then Loewe and Max Mara ("Thinking man's tourist-bait"), then labels for people who thought they had money but didn't—your Coaches, your Michael Kors. "Imagine wearing Michael Kors on purpose," Edith said. I told her that was a bad thing to say. "It is true, though," she said.

Whenever I wore something Julian had bought me, I felt Edith could tell what it cost and did not think it was worth the money.

We went to Zara. I asked why Zara was acceptable when Michael Kors was not, and Edith said it was because Zara knew who they were. She added that she was well aware on another level that this was all consumerist garbage, but Mrs. Zhang's influence was hard to shake off. "You're right," I said, "it is consumerist garbage." She smiled. I was glad she seemed to find my sullenness endearing, but suspected she only did because it did not much affect her. I pictured us as cartoon characters, me trying to headbutt her, stuck in the same spot with my forehead ramming into her serenely outheld palm.

At the racks she chose things for us to try on. I was too embarrassed to check if we were the same size, but Edith asked mine and said we were. She said it would save time if we shared a changing-room stall. I turned away and then Edith did the same, like it wouldn't otherwise have occurred to her. Through the mirror I saw her black lace bra. Her deodorant smelled like soap. "I like your freckles," she said, still with her back to me. She could have been admitting she'd glanced over her shoulder or could simply have been commenting on the parts of me she'd already seen, and I felt it wouldn't have killed her to be clearer about that.

"I like your dress," I said. "Mine is ugly." Edith said no, it was just different. It was the first time we'd disagreed on clothes. "The neck-line brings out your collarbones," she said. I told her she had nice collarbones, too, that wasn't it interesting we pluralized collarbones when it was really all one bone, and also that the dress was still ugly. "Let me try it on if you don't want it," she said. I took it off. This time I stayed facing her.

Later I started another Potemkin message to Julian.

i think i'm flirting with edith. she seems like someone who flirts with everyone, and so doesn't really flirt with anyone. i don't know what's happening. i've known her two months and it feels like she's the only person in my life who has ever mattered or existed.

I highlighted the text and pressed the back key, then navigated out and back into my drafts three times to make sure the deletion had been saved. In the now-empty box I wrote: i wish i knew how i felt about everything, then erased that, too.

———

Victoria invited me out for tea again, alluding to things Julian had "written to her about." "Writing" just meant "messaging," but made them sound in deeper cahoots. I replied that I was busy with work. I watched myself type this thing that would obviously make Victoria hate me even more than she already did, then kept watching as I pressed send.

Mam also said it had been a while. When I called, she said I seemed distracted. Julian messaged, then again a few days later saying—cockily, I thought—that it wasn't like me to take so long to reply. Even Tom asked if things were well. It was so long since we'd last spoken that I forgot to upbraid him for telling Mam about Julian.

Whenever I was waiting for Edith's replies, I touched my collarbone. Then she'd message.

The first Sunday of May, she and I went to a sushi place in Queensway. We met at the station and walked past money-changers and double-decker trams on Hennessy Road. The Chinese pharmacies smelled of scallops and woody ginseng. Edith saw me looking at the display crates of brown shriveled remedies, and said Mrs. Zhang had detailed thoughts on what worked and what didn't if I ever needed help.

"Birds' nests for coughs," she said.

I tried to jaywalk at a crossing, but she pulled me back.

The sushi restaurant had a conveyor belt. I didn't eat fish, so my options were limited. Edith saw a cucumber roll before I did, jerked forwards to grab it, then smiled in triumph at what a good provider she was. She rated me as an intermediate chopstick user. I wasn't embarrassing myself, but nor would I be winning prizes. When I couldn't follow her demonstration, she reached over and arranged the sticks in my hand. Afterwards I was scared to put them down in case I couldn't reposition them at the correct angle.

"How long do you think you'll stay in Hong Kong?" Edith said.

"I don't know," I said. "Maybe till I want to get a mortgage."

"If you don't mind my saying," she said, "your flat is quite nice. Maybe you could move somewhere cheaper."

"To be honest, Julian pays most of the rent."

"Really?" she said.

There was always surprise in Edith's voice. That was her charm.

But it made it harder to tell when a statement had genuinely non-plussed her. She held her chin at just that angle, and widened her eyes just so, to take in words, any words. This face was one of my favorites of Edith's, but its ubiquity muddled matters when I'd told her something difficult and didn't know what to say next.

"It's complicated," I said.

"This is none of my business," she said, "but—"

"Are you wondering—"

"Yes."

"No. But I don't mind you asking."

I wondered if I was being dishonest to avoid hurting my, quote, chances with her, end quote. But I didn't think that was it. I was un-scrupulous enough to lie so I could have sex with someone, but while I'd do other things just as bad, it wasn't the sort of bad thing I'd do. Unless, of course, I was telling myself that so I'd feel I was being duly self-critical, while remaining fuzzy on which of my behaviors ever did count as the sort of bad thing I'd do.

Also, I still didn't know Edith's sexuality. I thought about invent-ing an ex-girlfriend to see her reaction, but this felt beyond the pale. There was no limit to what I would trawl through online, and clearly none on the information I would hide from Edith, but I wouldn't make up a person. That was my moral purlieu. Coincidentally, bringing up a girlfriend would take courage, whereas cyberstalking was easy.

There was the question of Julian, but he'd laughed at me back in February when I asked if he minded me flirting with men. Women, I assumed, were fair game. Even if they weren't, I knew I'd keep seeing Edith anyway.

25

I tried to keep seeing Miles, not least so I would have some way to account to Julian how I was spending my time. It also distracted me from thinking about Edith, which was nice because then when I remembered her again, it felt better than the last time.

Miles told me about how Mao heeded the failed Taiping rebellion in the mid-nineteenth century. Like him, the Taipings imported a rebellious foreign doctrine. Unlike him, they never made it resonate with locals and so were crushed by the gentry's grassroots militia.

"Another reason Marxist academia shouldn't be a universe unto itself," said Miles. It was the fourth time I'd gone to see him since Julian's departure. "And between us," he said, "it makes me question the purpose of what I do. Who reads academics' books?"

"I have to admit I don't," I said—absent-mindedly, but he laughed and said he could always count on me for brutal honesty.

That wasn't true. I often lied to spare others' feelings or to make them like me. Most of my directness was by accident. But I got more social capital from pretending it was on purpose, not least because it made people assume my compliments had to be sincere. Julian seemed to trust me. Smart people often did dumb things.

"Would you like tea?" Miles said.

I thought it was too hot for that but said yes, then offered to make it myself. Miles declined twice and accepted the third time. The kitchenette had a window and poor soundproofing, so I heard and saw men in hats doing something with drills outside.

Miles said he was coming to prefer my company to Julian's. I knew that wasn't true but thanked him for saying it. I wondered if it was obvious how much I craved his son's approval, or if he thought everyone wanted Julian to like them. For some time, I'd been dying to ask him who'd come to Hong Kong first: father or son? I frequently pictured a conversation where one of them was already installed there, and then the other rang from England to announce they'd be moving over, too. They'd both remain calm on the surface, but the exchange would have far-reaching emotional implications. Julian would say "right" a lot.

I couldn't think of Julian for too long without cycling back to Edith. Most persons, places, and things led me her way, but Julian especially triggered it. I sat there in Miles's apartment and thought: Edith, and smiled.

—

"Drink faster, Irish," Edith said.

"You know it's a serious social problem in Ireland?"

"Yeah, okay. Sorry. Drink moderately."

We'd picked up Ladies' Night champagne at a rooftop bar in LKF on a Friday in mid-May. The premise of the evening was that bars gave us free drinks so we'd stay there for men to sleaze on. Edith said this made girl-on-girl dating quite affordable for the savvy consumer. I couldn't remember if most women made jokes like Edith's, or how their faces looked when they did make them.

We were getting mullered before Cyril Kwok's twenty-third. Edith asked if "mullered" meant what she thought it did. Yes, I said. Irish English made sense. That was how one distinguished it from British English.

"Anyway," I said, "why do we need to get mullered?"

"You'll see," Edith said.

"Ar meisce is the Irish Irish."

"Let's get ar meisce," she said, as if deciding to keep it.

The Ladies' Night champagne was a shoddy payment for talking to the men. Anything would be. They slapped the tables whenever anyone said anything, which seemed, bizarrely, to encourage them all to say more. You would need to drink a huge amount not to deliberately step on their foot, and the quality of the alcohol did not lend itself to this.

We'd claimed wicker chairs in the corner. Edith drank three flutes of champagne in ten minutes. I asked if she really needed that much sedation for Cyril Kwok's.

"He Instagrams his friends' car keys," Edith said. "They pile their keys on the coffee table, and he posts a picture and tags them."

"As in, he tags them as their keys?" I said.

Edith rolled her eyes, like: no, he tags them as the post-fact malaise.

It was my turn to top up our drinks. "And one for my friend," I said to the barman, enunciating sternly to tell him he could take from that just what he wanted.

Back at the rooftop, Edith was answering emails on her phone. I stood at a distance for some time, as though waiting for something to change. When I came and put the flutes on the table, I said—feeling I could if I was doing something else while saying it—that I wondered if women ever did use Ladies' Night for dates.

"It's certainly a strategy," she said.

No one could be good at Edith.

She hailed a taxi and swapped sentences with the driver in Cantonese. In the cab I slipped my heels off and felt the carpet through my tights.

"Taxis always smell like new car," I said.

"They use a spray," Edith said.

"You know everything."

"You're ar meisce."

She stroked a ladder on my tights and said I should be more careful. I wondered if this was a simple extension of her domain over everything, or if I'd somehow indicated she was allowed. I'd said I was
hers from how I looked at her—not from how I'd chosen to look at her,
but from how I couldn't help looking at her—but that didn't mean she
could tell. Maybe Edith didn't notice me at all and touched me as she
would a small appliance.

The taxi dropped us uphill and we passed three checkpoints
through to a marble lobby with a twenty-foot fig tree in the center.
There were potted bonsais on all conducive surfaces, including one in
the lift. Edith said having children was like growing bonsai. I asked
what growing a full-size tree was like. That, Edith said, was a question of temperament.

Cyril Kwok met us at the door. He wore white from head to toe:
sweatshirt, jeans, trainers. "Pick a color," he said.

"This is Ava," Edith said.

"Hi, Ava. Pick a color."

"Pink," I said. "Hi, Cyril."

"Rosé it is."

The party was loud and dark, with flashing lights. Cyril led us
through the atrium and up the mezzanine to what he called "the
bucket." I was relieved to see it was an actual bucket. He fished inside
and found Edith a bottle of Armand de Brignac. "Happy me turning
twenty-three," he said, kissing cheeks before excusing himself.

I told Edith he seemed nice and asked why she hated him. She
didn't hear me the first time, so I had to say it into her ear.

"I thought you'd judge me for liking him," she said. "He went to
Eton."

"Julian went to Eton," I said.

Edith gripped the rosé as though to remind me she held the talking stick. "You always bring up Julian," she said.

I hadn't been sure she was drunk until then.

"You shouldn't pretend you hate your friends," I said. The noise drowned me out again and Edith asked me to repeat myself, which let me redraft it to: "Sorry I made you feel like you have to pretend to hate your friends."

Edith had to catch up with everyone and I didn't, so she considered who to leave me with. I was too used to this from Julian to mind. "I'll give you to Tony Ng," she decided. "He was at Wadham, so he tries not to act rich now." Edith looked over at Tony's red chinos as though to tell me I could judge for myself his success in this.

"Ling Ling, you're glowing," Tony said. "How's Sam?"

"We broke up," Edith said.

"Wow," Tony said. "It's been eons."

"Definite eons," Edith said.

With a clarity I blamed on alcohol, I knew precisely what I felt: envy. It was partly that Edith's friends were rich, but mainly that she had them. The Sam thing I would get to later.

"This is Ava," Edith told Tony. "Ava's single."

"Me, too," Tony said. "Let's see which of us gets a man first."

I could reply: or a woman. But I didn't know if Edith had introduced me to Tony thinking it might prompt my disclosure, or if the possibility had never occurred to her. The girls at school had claimed to want a gay best friend, despite not being someone any gay would want to be friends with. They still called me all sorts of things for not kissing enough boys.

Edith and Tony had changed the subject now, so I nodded and made engaged expressions. I saw I hadn't just been holding back from coming out to Edith as part of some game. I also feared that she'd stop being friends with me. I thought that about Julian, too, and about anyone in my life who had ever remotely cared about me, but I'd never had to confront it in Hong Kong because I hadn't had a crush on a woman till now. Or maybe I didn't care about coming out and just didn't want her to know that I was into her specifically. It was impossible to separate these issues. I couldn't like Edith without liking women, and I also felt—illogically, but with conviction—that

I couldn't like women without liking Edith. And I had that thought mid-laugh, so I had to keep laughing or Edith would see what I'd been thinking.

———

That night at home I searched Edith's friend list online. There were six Sams: four male, two female. I clicked "see friendship" between Edith and me, then went to the URL and edited my account name to each of the Sams in turn so it showed their history with her. Three of them—two men, one woman—had nothing but birthday wall posts. One was only tagged with Edith in group pictures from Cambridge. The last pair, he-Sam and she-Sam, each had a single photo with their arm around her.

26

I turned twenty-three on May 18. The other teachers asked me along to the pub, but I said, truthfully, that I had plans. I'd asked Edith out for once and hadn't told her it was my birthday. I was embarrassed by the idea that she'd think I thought we were closer friends than we were. She texted me a balloon emoticon on the morning, which made me wonder if she'd known all along what day it was or if she'd just got a notification about it.

We met at a whiskey bar on Hollywood Road. Edith's present to me was a printed scarf by an LA-based eco-feminist collective. I was skeptical of its claimed carbon neutrality when it had been shipped from California to Hong Kong, but it was soft against my neck—and it was wrapped, which suggested she'd known it was my birthday.

We went inside. The place was crowded. The menu asked: would you make a pact with heaven for the finest drink on earth?

Edith found the Irish section and ordered me a Connemara peated single malt. "Shipped from the old country," I said. "Bring a tear to the eye, so it would." When it arrived, it was so strong it actually did. She said I was a baby and then shuddered herself when she tried it. Julian had called me that once, a baby, and I felt this proved that words took their meaning from context.

Next we had cider. Mid-gesticulation, I knocked my glass over and spilled some on my lap. She took out pocket tissues. I thought she'd hand me one, but she leaned over and dabbed my thigh. Her hair smelled of smoke from the walk through LKF.

Edith addressed the waiter in English, but he answered in Cantonese.

"He guessed right," she said after he'd gone away, "but I could have been from anywhere."

"Maybe he doesn't speak English," I said. It was a stupid comment, but I wanted to distract myself from her pout. It was another of my favorite Edith expressions, though I knew there was limited point in recording them when I could not imagine a single expression of Edith's which did not rank among my favorites. The best wedges of words were the ones my eight-year-olds wrote: I like her face. With her I am happy. I wished I'd never learned more advanced grammar and could only make sentences like that. It would give me an excuse to say them aloud.

"You're not noticing because you're white," Edith said. "People see me and assume I'm from here."

"But you are from here."

"Kind of," she said. "But you miss things when you spend your teens abroad."

It sounded like something a therapist might have told her, oddly phrased to squeeze developmental insight into not very many words.

She added that many people, her parents included, had a misplaced nostalgia for the British Empire because at least it wasn't China. "Hong Kong is the one place where the late-twentieth-century rebrand has worked," she said. We both found it hilarious that Brits thought their international image was one of flaccid tea-loving Hugh Grantish butterfingery. If they'd been a bit more indirect during the Opium Wars, or a bit more self-effacing on Bloody Sunday, then our countries would have been most appreciative. "That's why they can't accept that they did colonialism," Edith said. "They see themselves as people who can't even get a dog put down." We agreed also that the British obsession with dogs was creepy, both because of the volume of other animals they ate and in light of their historic and contemporary level of regard for humans.

We talked fast together. I was always slowing down in Hong Kong, either to help the kids understand me or because Julian said everything at leisure and I felt I should stay in rank. Only with Edith could my mouth get ahead of me. The other mercy was that in the thick of assertion I could pretend not to notice her knee against mine.

We did shots, then went down Aberdeen Street to the pier. It was too late to get a decent view, but she said she liked watching the boats and imagining their shapes by drawing lines between the lights like a join-the-dots. Our walk started with ignoring everyone around us and ended with no one to ignore.

"You know," Edith said, "it used to be illegal for locals to live on the Peak. I'm not sure about Mid-Levels, but definitely the Peak."

"Why?" I said. "Who lived there?"

She laughed. "The British, of course."

I wanted her to give me one of her spiels, with her gestures like bodily extensions of her facts, but she left it there. It was 9 p.m. The office buildings sported a few dark windows like punched-out options on a game show, but plenty still burned bright. I pictured a thousand Ediths and Julians hunched over tables, hitting targets, making waves, spitting out productivity. In front of us, though, the water held still.

"I wonder if there's a time in Hong Kong when not a single person is working," I said.

Edith turned to me slowly. "I hate my job," she said. "I work hard, it's good to work hard, but I hate it. I just want my mum to be proud of me. Which is stupid, because the things she values aren't the things I value, but she's my mum. I care what she thinks."

"Just tell yourself you're doing it ironically," I said.

"Do people still say that?" Edith said.

I cast for sincerity.

"I like girls," I said. Then: "I like you."

She kissed me.

27

We texted throughout the following week. I did it at work, or while walking around shopping malls. I tried to wait fifteen minutes. I'd write in the notepad app to stop her from seeing me type, count the seconds, then cut, paste, and send. But I soon found once I'd written something, I needed to show her right away.

Among these messages: so do you want to get coffee or something?

The three elliptic minutes watching her type had a gravitational field all their own. She did not want to get coffee or something, or anything. The kiss, you see, was done in pastiche. Why was she taking this long to say no? Just say it and leave me for the worms to find.

Then: yes, i'd like that.

We got specialty coffees in Sheung Wan and laughed as we drank them. Mine was charcoal with cashew milk and hers was bright pink dragonfruit. I considered asking if this made me the man, but decided ironic heteronormativity was still heteronormative, and also that it was too early to make that joke.

I wondered which was better: a first date after three months of knowing someone, or moving into their apartment after three but still being "friends" with them half a year later. Neither seemed wildly successful, but I was too happy about Edith to mind.

I couldn't focus at work. I would sit correcting papers, then think of her and cross my legs tighter together. In class the children asked me what words meant or whether a spelling was correct. Instead of making them use the dictionary like I was meant to, I just told them the answer. It was fine. They had smartphones. Through the walls I heard the other teachers giving stern instructions, and wondered if my problem was that I didn't want to teach like they did, or that I didn't want to be a teacher at all.

I hated being in charge. I wanted Edith to tell me what we were and how it worked. Whenever Julian did that, I hadn't liked the answer. It struck me now that maybe I could have—for instance—told him that, with words, instead of pretending to be okay with it. Then I felt glad to have a new chance. I'd lied to Edith, too, but not as consistently, and not about how I felt.

My favorite students were the girls with neat copybooks. I knew they'd grow up to be like Edith, and was glad Hong Kong had a long-term supply. Connie Qian kept glue and a small pair of scissors in her pencil case. She cut out choice paragraphs from my handouts and stuck them in her notepad. "I like your notebooks," I told her. Then I wondered if I should have said it more bossily to make it clear that I was not trying—ever—to be anyone's pal. Connie considered, then accepted my praise. "I like them," she said—no "too," perhaps to show her judgment was independent of mine. This also seemed like something Edith would do.

No student had ever reminded me of Julian. Despite my speculations about his background, I'd never been able to picture him as an actual child. He didn't want me to see him any way other than how he was now. He liked me because I didn't know him before he was on a six-figure salary.

I asked Edith over to the flat a week after our first date. Unusually, she wore jeans and a cable-knit jumper. She presented me with a diamond-patterned crystal bowl for the coffee table and said to fill it with fruit or flowers. At face value it was obviously a gift for me, but the fact that Edith had handpicked it for Julian's apartment made me uncertain what to say. Were we grateful, or just me?

We ate fruit and watched an old film with Judy Garland. I wondered if other people watched movies when they asked someone around to do that, or if our actually doing it meant things were going horribly wrong.

"I find Judy's brow intriguing," said Edith. "It's owlish."

We were less taken with the plot. Judy was a dowdy farmer whose wayfaring actress sister set up camp in her barn to rehearse jaunty musical numbers with her troupe. There was a predictable dalliance with the sister's dashing fiancé, but we forgave him for being formulaic because he was played by Gene Kelly. Had the technology existed, I was sure Gene would not have got this far into a movie when he asked a woman around to watch one.

"Do you think she's pretty?" said Edith.

"Judy?"

"Of course."

Edith could have meant "of course" because who else could I possibly find attractive, or "of course" because Judy, as both an LGBT icon and person of a gender I'd broadly said I liked, was a woman I was especially likely to have opinions on.

"I see where you're coming from about the owlish brow," I said. "And she's got a good profile on her. She and Gene have a great pair of noses."

There were better things I could have said—I regretted involving Gene, who really had no stake in this—but she kissed me anyway.

"Judy's great," she said. "The studio made her wear prosthetics on her nose, you know. But I don't think she has them on here. She put her foot down in the end."

"I wish you wouldn't kiss me and then go off about Judy Garland's prosthetic nose."

"I told you, it's not prosthetic, it's her actual one."

"Look," I said. We started kissing again and I forgot what I'd wanted her to consider.

There was a Pavlovian moment where I started leading her towards Julian's room, but I stopped and brought her to mine instead. We went down on each other. She grabbed at my hair and said: yes, right there. Afterwards we compared our bodies, and I realized that I had never actually felt calm doing it before. Now I could relax. Our limbs didn't seem to belong to either of us in particular. Edith had longer arms, we agreed.

"I'm so happy," I said.

"Me, too," she said.

I asked if the taste was all right. I'd always wanted to ask Julian, but knew what he'd say: "Fine," which would make me worry more, or: "Like Pinot Noir, but I'm not sure if that's because you've had some or I have." Edith said she couldn't describe it. I found myself breathing artificially slowly, as though to placate someone else, and realized it wasn't the answer I was interested in. It was being able to say I felt anxious.

She had to go. Her parents expected her home. I told myself this had nothing to do with my question potentially being weird, then recollected that if she'd said something odd then I would almost certainly wait a bit and say other things before leaving.

There was no record of what had happened. I couldn't fully believe in it when it hadn't been committed to paper. Maybe that was why Sappho wrote poems—but when she died, they wrapped her papyrus around corpses to keep maggots off.

It was fortunate Edith had left before I'd started waxing existential. I told myself: This is why you're single. This is how you can be having sex with two people, tell neither about the other, be living with one of them, and still be single.

28

JUNE

At the start of June my nine-year-olds finished irregular plural and compound nouns, and moved on to collectives: a flock of sheep, a clutch of eggs, a shower of wankers. The latter I kept to myself, but I did wonder what the English said, because it couldn't be a "shower of," but as a fundamentally onanistic nation they surely had some way to cluster it. I thought about how to ask Edith and make it funny as opposed to weird, and then Kendrick Yang asked what you said for grapes and I lost my train of thought. "Bunch," I said, "—no, cluster," and then I doubted myself again. He'd already written "cluster," so I left it there.

Sometimes I wondered if I was actually a native English speaker. As a kid I'd daydreamed about having been secretly adopted from a foreign country. Russia was the leading candidate since I'd read a historical novel about a family fleeing the October Revolution, though I knew if I revisited the book now I would think it had terrible politics. Books about people who lost their money, or had none and got some, appealed more to my childhood imagination than ones where everyone stayed put—though that was far more common in real life. And characters who didn't consider class at all were boring. I couldn't believe those people existed. Everyone in school knew who had the biggest houses and whose parents were barristers.

I'd once explained "on the scratcher" and "in the scratcher" to Julian and asked if he thought there was something about the Irish character discernible from the near indistinguishability of drawing the dole and going to bed with someone. He'd been sleepy and hadn't said much. I wondered if I could nab this observation and see what Edith made of it, but knew I'd feel wrong. I wasn't sure, though, if the guilt would be for repeating something Julian thought I'd only say to him, or for tendering Edith old rope.

It was Julian's fourth month away now. I felt on some level like he'd never come back.

———

Edith and I kept having sex. There was only one feeling better than being chosen by someone so perfect, and that was having her utter the sentence: "I want you to finger me."

Most people had crevices of soft skin—behind ears, wrists, under sleeves—but all of Edith's felt like that. She was so small it felt comically unnecessary to hold her close. We'd wrap around each other and laugh at how much bed we had left. I saw myself telling people: we always make room for each other, for you see we are compact. Then I remembered that I'd just spent half a year having quite a lot of sex with a vertically bothersome man. It was all very interesting.

When Edith wasn't busy working, we'd lie in my bed sharing secrets. After three weeks of this, she said she'd always been exclusively into girls, but it took her until Cambridge to realize not all women were and that this made her gay.

I asked if she'd ever tell her family.

"No," she said instantly.

I claimed I'd tell mine if I ended up with a woman. Until then, there was no need to apprise them of my sex life. "Not that it's all about sex," I said. "But that's what they'd boil it down to."

Edith agreed. Ninety percent of why she couldn't tell her parents was the sex thing.

I'd never slept with a woman before, though I'd spent most of my teens and college years obsessed with one or another. They'd all had boyfriends, or girlfriends, or else they were just patently not someone who would ever fancy me. When I told Edith this, she asked if I thought I'd gone for unavailable people because I knew I'd never have to face the reality that being with them would not solve all my problems. I told her she had no business saying something that perceptive.

"Everyone does that, Ava," she said. "You keep describing yourself as this uniquely damaged person, when a lot of it is completely normal. I think you want to feel special—which is fair, who doesn't—but you won't allow yourself to feel special in a good way, so you tell yourself you're especially bad."

I asked her again to stop reading me so well, and she laughed and said: "Fine, I tried." But really I liked when she psychoanalyzed me. Her air of knowledgeable objectivity reassured me that someone had the situation—me—in hand.

She'd had sex before with her ex at Cambridge—Sam, she said. It was easier then. Their whole circle was LGBT. She'd edged back into the closet since returning to Hong Kong.

"Sam," I repeated, to show it was new information.

We were too self-conscious to kiss in public. The first time had been permissible because it was spontaneous, but once it became a pattern, we worried people would notice. Small gestures took on significance. I'd nudge her on the arm to look at something on my phone. We went back to Central Pier and took a selfie, and I sent her it with the caption: just gals being pals. I put a picture of Edith on my Instagram story, and when I saw that Julian had seen it, I felt a twinge that I thought at first was fear, but which I realized was more like excitement. Neither of them had all my secrets.

———

At work I pretended I was her, or that she was watching me. When the children whispered or watched videos on their phones, instead of ignoring it like I usually did, I coughed the way I knew Edith would. It worked. They stopped. When Clarice Xu asked me for help, I told her she was doing great. I didn't usually think of myself as someone who could dispense compliments freely. They wouldn't interest anyone. But you didn't need to be that great for a ten-year-old to want your approval, and it helped that I had the blackboard markers and they didn't.

Sometimes Edith came to meet me after work at the train station nearby. I was allowed to touch her then. We could stand on an escalator and I could reach out and do it. It was a normal thing for friends to do. I wanted people to know we were together, but only the ones who wouldn't hurt us for it. I'd have felt afraid to in Dublin, and I did in Hong Kong, too.

I wanted to explain that to Edith: that holding Julian's hand was like holding a museum pass, and holding hers was like holding a grenade. But that didn't make sense even in my head, so I knew it wouldn't if I tried to say it aloud. And she didn't want to hold hands either, so it never came up.

I saw Miles again in June. He told me about the future communist leader Zhou Enlai hiding from machine-gun fire and bayonets at the Western Astor House Hotel in Guangzhou. To blend in, Zhou and his wife wore (respectively) a three-piece suit and a silk qipao dress. The anti-communist General Chiang knew they were there but most likely let them go to repay the time Zhou had saved him from violent leftists. I felt it would have been a better story if I'd known more about the figures involved.

Miles also told me about Julian's birth, then about when he'd met Florence. She'd had a smart pencil skirt on and said she worked at the Bank of England. He'd asked if she was a secretary, and she'd said no, that she was a policy adviser and was saving up to do a PhD. "You must forgive me," said Miles. "Those were different times. She forgave me, at any rate." He looked like he wanted to add that she did hold plenty of other grudges.

Since I'd started visiting when Julian left, Miles seemed to be dropping in more snippets of their family life. It felt unfair that this was happening only now that my top priority was not finding out more about Julian.

We listened to one of Nina Simone's 1976 Montreux recordings, "I Wish I Knew How It Would Feel to Be Free." Miles said it had been a sixties civil rights anthem in the US. Nina sang: I wish I could say all the things I can say when I'm relaxed.

It was no good trying to finish writing his book at the moment, Miles said. Instead, he was trying to devote more attention to his undergrads. There'd been a lot of students in the Umbrella protests a few years ago, and that kind of thing was needed more and more.

"So you want to brainwash your class?" I said.

"Yes. While I still can."

"My eight-year-olds are mad into conspiracy theories. Do you want a go with them?"

Nina sang: Jonathan Livingston Seagull ain't got nothing on me.

I looked at my watch and counted fifteen minutes without thinking about Edith, a personal record. Obviously, though, this set me off again. Miles had asked what I'd been up to, and I hadn't known what to say because I'd been spending all my time with Edith. I didn't mind Miles knowing, but if I told him about Edith then Julian might find out. If he found out about Edith, maybe Edith would find out about him. Then she'd want to know why I'd been lying. "I lie to everyone about everything" would probably not satisfy her as an answer.

29

In mid-June, Edith said we'd get boring—"As people," she said, a qualification I later analyzed stringently—if we just had sex all the time. I said I disagreed, but that we could go on dates if it made her happy. "It does," Edith said. I was still so unused to her candor that it threw me into admitting I liked dating, too. "A lot of people do," she said. I said I pitied anyone who didn't.

We got street food and bet on horses at Happy Valley. She took me for bubble tea on a long hilly street packed with convenience stores, and made fun of how long I took choosing, and then of my choice. ("If you hadn't rushed me, I might have chosen better." "Anyone who picks 'Matcha Love Potion,' in any allotted time period, is a threat to public safety.") We tried—and failed, but, importantly, tried—to get me over my fear of heights on the Hong Kong Observation Wheel, and the Lantau Island cable car up over the mountains. On both I screamed and grabbed Edith's hand, realized it was a coupley thing to do, and wondered if other people did coupley things and then questioned their own sincerity. But even if everyone else did the same things Edith and I did on dates, I decided it was still special for us.

One day we went to Man Mo Temple to make a wish. Incense smoked from ceiling coils. We stood at the urn, round and gold like a chalice, and I asked Edith what I wanted. "You tell me," she said. I laughed and kissed her cheek.

The last week of June, Edith asked when Julian would return.

"I don't know," I said. "He's vague."

We'd just been shopping. Julian had told me I could get more throws after I said I liked the one in my room. I'd bought four with Edith, two in herringbone and two in windowpane, and was arranging them in the sitting room. Edith hadn't said much about my choices, causing me to suspect that she hated them, and that Julian would, too, when he got back. It was unfair that they both had better taste than me.

I added: "Do you think the throws are boring?"

"Vague how?" Edith said. "The throws are fine."

It was all on stolen time and I'd pay later. I knew that. My temple wish had been for Julian to come back and for it all to be fine. But I couldn't imagine it with any precision. I'd close my eyes and see him greet her, and that was as far as I could get.

Whenever Edith was busy, I went out and walked my circuits of convenience stores and shopping malls, or I stayed in bed doing nothing. I wasn't lonely. My job was nonstop human contact, so I appreciated the time alone. But I couldn't quite relax.

That night I messaged Julian: i miss you. This was a strange thing to do.

———

I wanted to improve my handwriting so I could set a better example for my students. I found a French cursive font online, then wrote out sentences containing every letter of the alphabet: the quick brown fox jumps over the lazy dog, pack my box with five dozen liquor jugs, amazingly few discotheques provide jukeboxes. This seemed like a punishment, though I wasn't sure what for. After exhausting my supply of pangrams, I copied out Shakespeare sonnets.

While we were watching a movie in bed, Edith saw one of my transcriptions in a notebook on my bedside table. She said I had lovely handwriting. I felt bad for accepting the compliment, like the letters on the page weren't really mine.

That week my ten-year-olds did "if" and "whether." I'd known that in French you needed to use similar words when you turned a question into a noun clause, but Dubliners didn't always bother. We often said, "I don't know will he come back," which was bad English. You were meant to say: I don't know whether he'll come back, or: I don't know if he will.

I underlined the conjunctions in the example sentences, then set the kids to work. A few finished early and chatted in Cantonese. I pretended not to notice.

Ollie from Melbourne came in to borrow a whiteboard marker. We talked while the children wrote. In his most pedagogical voice, Ollie told me conjunctions were tricky buggers. There was a knack to them, he said, hooking his hand as though the knack was floating and he'd undertaken to catch it for me.

Julian hadn't replied to my "i miss you." I wondered if I really did, or if I'd wanted to feel powerful by claiming something about myself that wasn't true and which would trick him into thinking he had the upper hand. I didn't do things like that with Edith. It wasn't that I was more authentically myself around her. Manipulation was a part of my character or I wouldn't do it. But Edith didn't bring it out, and Julian did. I didn't like who I was around him, but I felt I had to be that person sometimes because they were bad and I was bad.

"You keep yourself to yourself, Ava," Ollie said. It was apropos of something, but I'd tuned out. I said I had a lot on my mind.

───

Finally Julian replied to the message about missing him. He'd taken so long I'd nearly forgotten I'd sent it.

Sorry—busy at work. Miss you too.

I felt disloyal to Edith when it made me smile, then to Julian because it was the kind of text Edith sent every day and I still appreciated it more from her than from him. This contravened all economics. Assuming my demand for nice messages was elastic, when they were scarcer it should surely drive up their value. But coming from Edith, they commanded a premium.

————

Edith and I talked a lot during sex. Julian had never been verbal in bed, which had made it embarrassing when I was, like I'd misunderstood what we were trying to do. With Edith, speech was part of it— slipping, getting words out till we couldn't. She said: keep going, we've got ages. When we finished I said that was weird, and also a little depressing, like: let's not hold back sexually since we're still relatively far from our anticipated time of death. Edith said: (a) she'd meant the last train wasn't for a few hours, and (b) if we were going to start calling each other out on bizarre coital utterances then let's not even.

We continued to hold Judy Garland in the esteem which was her due. "I found a picture of her in her fifties," Edith said. "We were right about the strigine brow. She looks unflappable. Not in a placid way, in like a tough-old-broad way."

"That chimes with her personal history."

"We should visit her grave," Edith said.

"You're always so morbid after we have sex," I said. "I can't help drawing inferences."

My "always" had no business describing something we'd only been doing a few weeks. I saw Edith register and approve of its reifying effect.

Sometimes I'd imagine her at Cambridge. I didn't know why I did that. My dinner-with-Florence reveries were probably not the sort of thing happy people thought about, but at least served an obvious purpose. The Cambridge thing didn't. But I liked seeing Edith's dark hair against the snow, or the stairs she'd climb in stone towers to get to tutorials. I thought about her life in Hong Kong, too. The Zhangs ate big dinners on national holidays, and the law firm I could reconstruct from its similarities to Julian's bank. I'd never seen the bank either, but had asked him to describe it.

Maybe I was living through Edith. When I planted her in high-flying venues, it was because I couldn't sow myself there and she was the next best thing. Vicarious aspiration couldn't quite explain why I was hooked on her life, but I didn't know myself well enough to get any closer.

"I found it scary in Ireland," I told her in my bed, "having sex with men."

I was really telling her that "I miss you" meant more from her than from Julian. It was not a link she could humanly be expected to make, which was why I could say it.

30

The last Sunday of June, we bought salads in Marks & Spencer and took the bus to Tai Pak Beach at Discovery Bay.

I liked getting the minibus with Edith. It was green and white, and jostled us violently. Even Edith dropped her sunglasses when it turned a corner. One evening there was no button and we had to shout at the driver to stop. Edith practiced the Cantonese with me—bus-ee jau m'goi—then made me call it out and laughed when I got the tones wrong.

It was hot on the beach. Three old ladies sat near us in foldout deck chairs with a parasol propped in the middle. I asked Edith what they were talking about, and she said they were speaking Hakka so she couldn't make much out. Edith's Singaporean grandmother was a native Hakka speaker and maintained you didn't need any other language in Hong Kong. There were some unfortunates who didn't speak it—indeed, a great many and perhaps more of them than one would like—but Mrs. Tan doubted it would improve their lot one whit if she dragged herself down to their level.

"Basically," Edith said, "my gran is the Hakka version of a British expat."

I knew I'd later repackage that comment as my own and send it to

Julian. Keeping up with both of them took work, but their similarities lent the enterprise a certain economy of scale. Not only could I regift my own observations to both of them, they enjoyed each other's without realizing who I'd stolen them from.

Edith asked me to teach her Irish. When she repeated the phrases, she didn't say them with her usual accent but with a Sinophone intonation. She said maybe it didn't matter how many languages you learned. You always brought the flavor of your first.

"Anyway, in fifty years we'll be speaking Mandarin," I said. "If you believe Julian. He says most of the clients are mainlanders now."

"Why have they kept him on?"

"He's very tall."

Edith said he sounded like a guy from her firm she went running with. He was an overpronating arsehole, she said. Overpronating was when your foot moved too far inward as it landed on the ground. Arsehole was when you had a personality like his.

"So why do you run with him?" I said.

"He's on my team at work, so it's that or drink beer with him."

Edith could make most words sound cutting, and "beer" was one such word.

"Do you think he has a crush on you?" I said.

"Men never fancy me," she said complacently.

"I think Julian might when he gets back. I'll have to warn him you're a lesbian. Have I shown you his ex?"

We looked at pictures of Kat. The screen glared in the sun. Edith said Kat was gorgeous and questioned how on earth Julian had convinced her to go out with him. "But I don't know him, so I shouldn't be uncharitable," she added, not necessarily in a tone of regret.

Then Edith asked if I thought I'd ever leave Hong Kong.

The Hakka ladies were watching, so I just stroked her hand. "We could leave together," I said. "London has law firms."

"I've heard there's a hiring freeze coming. Brexit and all that. And why London?"

"I don't know. It seems livable."

"Because it's away from your family?"

"Probably."

"I think you like your space," Edith said.

I couldn't say: everyone in Dublin hated me, such that I came to hate myself, too, and I came out here trying to change that and it'd kind of worked but not fully. I didn't think Edith would get it. I also wasn't sure if it was even true about everyone hating me. It had felt that way, but maybe it did for everyone at that age.

She went back to a document on her iPad, and I considered what I'd said about us leaving together. It had just come out. I'd never really given it much thought. I could barely think about what might happen whenever Julian came back, let alone afterwards. But I could see us living somewhere very tidy, and neither of our families ever finding out. The worst thing would be being out to hers but not to mine. It would give her more power: she'd be able to talk to them about me. Then I felt like a horrible person for wanting her relationship with her parents to be as secretive as mine just because it would keep us even. I wondered if other people had to consciously expel thoughts like that, or if they just never had them in the first place. But it was presumptuous to think about any of that. Probably I was jinxing the whole thing.

That night in Julian's apartment, I said: "Is it true there are loads of lesbians at boarding school?"

"If there are, they don't come out," said Edith. "The teachers were worried there wasn't enough compulsory heterosexuality, so they made us do socials with Eton."

I was about to say she might have bumped into Julian, then remembered he'd have started at Oxford by the time she came to the UK.

"No one was out in my year either," I said. "You'd have got a door slammed on you."

She looked at me like she didn't know if I was joking. I wasn't sure either. There were reasons besides men I'd been unhappy in Dublin.

Next morning, we walked in Sun Yat Sen Park. Edith asked how she could become my girlfriend. She said: "Is there a process involved?"

———

Julian messaged from London about Hong Kong politics. He knew more than I did. He asked if I'd heard that the High Court had upheld a gay civil servant's spousal benefits. It might go to the Court of Appeal, but was watershed stuff all the same. An Aussie at his bank was out, but no locals he knew. Maybe things would change now. During this conversation I was especially grateful not to have to keep my face arranged.

I asked how he found it back in England. He wrote:

Mum's happy I'm here. Happier if I quit my job but she's accepted I won't. Some people married now, which should be illegal. Don't know why anyone's proud of having found someone. Statistically likelier than not that they will, particularly if they lower their standards. And someone from Balliol is having a baby. I suppose the world needs people to have babies.

We chose what to share. Through composition I reduced my life, burned fat, filed edges. The editing process let me veto post hoc the painful, boring, or irrelevant moments I lived through. Necessarily Julian curated what he told me, and that, too, made me happy. Together we were making something small and precise.

There was one area of my life I didn't tell him about that was neither painful nor boring nor irrelevant, but I saw other grounds for excluding it.

31

E dith had me over to meet her family on the second-to-last day of June. "Will it not be weird?" I said. "I presume they still don't know." Edith said it was fine. They'd be much more suspicious if they thought she was hiding me from them.

"Besides," she said, "it's been over a month. You can't not meet them."

The fact that "over a month" brought Edith and me into meeting-the-family territory, whereas I had known Julian for months before he'd even mentioned Miles, told me all I needed to know about dating gay women versus straight men.

The Zhangs' apartment was in Happy Valley, a residential area at the high altitude I had come to expect from rich people's homes. The floors were treacherous with polish. There were oil paintings propped against the walls, as if the Zhangs had bought them on a whim and would get around sooner or later to hanging them. On the shelves and side tables stood plain figurines: swans, stallions, elks. Edith explained that Mr. Zhang had got from somewhere the idea that Mrs. Zhang collected porcelain. She didn't, and scolded him for never remembering, but displayed it anyway so people would see that her husband was thoughtful.

Above the TV was a large framed photograph of a toddler in a gown and mortarboard. I assumed it was Edith at a ceremony for child geniuses, but she told me it was her sister at her kindergarten graduation, which everyone did—except Edith, who'd thrown up in the car and refused to go in. That evening Mrs. Zhang took Edith to see the principal and give a rehearsed apology for her absence. Mrs. Shek squinted and said: "Thank you, Edith—but, Mrs. Zhang, this wasn't necessary," and all the way home Mrs. Zhang said: "Wasn't necessary!" sometimes alternating with "Unnecessary!" for syllabic texture.

We watched TV. At the ad break Edith read out posts from her friend Audrey, a micro-influencer. Sometimes she showed her boyfriend's wallet in brunch flatlays, but never his face. That way when she switched boyfriends the brand endured.

We wondered about the straights.

"They're like pandas," Edith said. "You pity them in the zoo, but fling the cage open and they'll stay there, chewing."

"You know there's nothing intrinsically radical about us both being women."

"No, not intrinsically"—as if to say: challenge accepted.

She added that her mother would be back soon. "Don't mention the facelift," she said.

Mrs. Zhang entered. I didn't mention the facelift. She'd come home from grocery shopping with their helper, Cristina, who was a head shorter than she was and wore a T-shirt and track shorts. Mrs. Zhang told Edith she was getting fat, then ordered the maid to make us dumplings. The china was painted with leaves and flowers. While we ate, Cristina stood there refilling our water. Edith and Mrs. Zhang acted like this was normal, so I did, too. That's good to know about me, I thought. It's good to know how I behave in this situation.

Mrs. Zhang told us about last night's charity gala, then looked at Edith, who asked obediently if *Tatler* had come. "Perhaps," said Mrs. Zhang, eyes cast upwards as though *Tatler*'s spirit hath moved her.

She didn't pay me much attention. She asked what I did, and when I said I taught TEFL, she had no further questions. I was grateful. It would have embarrassed us both if she'd pretended to take an interest in someone as unsuccessful as me. Briefly I contemplated standing up, yanking at the tablecloth, watching the silverware crash into Mrs. Zhang's lap, and yelling at her that she had no business giving Edith complexes. But it wasn't my place.

After dinner, Mrs. Zhang showed us her wedding photos. I could see the resemblance to Edith more clearly in them, either because their ages were similar or because Mrs. Zhang's face was as yet unmarked by surgical intervention. Mr. Zhang was handsome and wore thick eighties glasses. The couple looked favored by destiny, like the subjects of a glossy history-book picture taken before they were famous.

Mr. Zhang was in Guangzhou for the day. Edith said I'd meet him soon, and her sister, Gabrielle, and her brother, Angus, when he was back from New York, and her grandparents at some point of course, and then I'd have met the Zhangs.

———

The following evening, Edith and I went to see *Vampire Cleanup Department* at the Paterson Street cinema. The plot followed Tim Cheung, a Hong Kong student who became an orphan when his parents got bitten on an anti-vampire mission. As Edith said, it fulfilled the functions of a B-movie and if you expected anything else then you'd missed the point.

The light from the theater screen blinked against her profile. Her lips were slightly open and her neck was long and pale like the filament of an orchid. I nearly reached out to touch her face, but she looked so still in that suspended moment that I didn't want her to flinch. I mouthed: you're so beautiful. Then: I love you. Edith broke her pose to chuckle when a character swallowed the protagonist's iPhone. I laughed, too. Our eyes met and we couldn't stop. Someone coughed pointedly from several rows down, which only set us off again. She covered her mouth with her hands. She did that when she found something genuinely funny, but didn't when she was only laughing to be polite. I liked knowing that about her.

It was 2 a.m. when we left. Neither of us needed to state aloud that we'd walk instead of getting a taxi so we could discuss things privately in the night air.

"Thanks for—you know, my mum," Edith said.

"What?"

"For how you handled that."

"What did she do?"

"Just her, in general. She's so rude to Cristina and I act normal about it, like that'll make it less awkward. But it's not about social graces anyway. There's no way of treating her that would make her working conditions okay."

"Aren't working conditions part of how you treat someone?" I said. "That's why I hate Benny. It's not that he doesn't ask nicely. It's that he's not really asking."

"True."

We turned right on Yee Wo Street past cut-price perfumes and medicine shops. Four bovine Australian men trudged abreast in front of us. We silently agreed to weave around the blockade. One of them whistled at Edith. She glided ahead like she was declining him admission to the category of people she was willing to notice.

"Sometimes I imagine the conversation where I come out to my mum," Edith said. "When I can't get to sleep at night, I go through the script."

Like much of Edith's phrasing, this sounded slightly rehearsed, and I wondered if I gave her that same feeling of needing to prepare. I wanted to tell her she didn't need to, but felt this would only make her more self-conscious. On another level I liked that I could embarrass someone as flawless as Edith. I could hurt her. I didn't want to, but I could.

I didn't need to know how other women went about being together. I could see it forever, for us: walking through cities, laughing at things that weren't that funny.

A few meters down from the Shanghai Commercial Bank was a Yun Fat Pawn Shop. It was part of a chain. I'd seen another in Wan Chai. There were no windows, but you could see blurred colors through the frosted glass door. At the top of Pennington Street we crossed the China Congregational Church and a dwarfing Armani billboard. We waited at the lights, then marched forward with the crowd onto Leighton Road. Edith strode with such command that I stayed a step behind to watch her movements. She wore red suede point-toe flats. In a more private setting, I'd have heard them against the cement.

32

JULY

Dad was visiting his sister's family in New York. Mam said he sent his love. I found that strange because it wasn't like his being in the US was suddenly depriving me of his company. New York was probably closer to me than Dublin, if anything. While Mam talked I messaged my girlfriend, Edith, whom I was going out with.

"Sorry for not calling last night," I said. "I was having dinner with a friend."

"Which friend?" Mam said.

"You don't know her."

Mam's assumption that she'd already be acquainted with any friend of mine had started in Junior Infants and, seemingly, endured after I'd moved continent.

"What's her name?" Mam said.

"Edith."

"Would she be from Hong Kong?"

Because Edith was one of the few Hong Kong people I'd mentioned, Mam was disproportionately curious about her. I avoided revealing that Edith was a lawyer for much the same reason I'd regretted mentioning that Julian was a banker. Since I hadn't told Mam Edith was my friend when we were friends, and had now called her my friend when we were girlfriends, I would probably announce her as my girlfriend only when we got married.

I regretted letting myself think that far.

"Ava?"

"Sorry, what?"

Mam told me off for daydreaming and repeated that Tom had started an internship at a bank.

"Good on him," I said.

"He's a smart boy, Ava," as if that had anything to do with it. "Your father's proud of him. And George misses you"—this appended as if it flowed naturally from what had come before. "He doesn't say so, but that'd be him. Keeps everything bottled up. Your dad would be the same. It'd mean the world to them if you'd come back to visit."

Mam didn't ask for things on her own account.

"I'll think about it," I said.

I knew I owed them a week back, but I wanted to wait until Julian returned. One of us needed to stay in Hong Kong to anchor our connection. The apartment was nautically high up, closer to the sky's amassed water than to anywhere roots grew, and it needed steady witnessing. If I left, everything between us would drift. Worse: it would remain, but I wouldn't see it.

"The Edith one," said Mam, "she's welcome to come and stay with us."

That would be a spectacle: Edith's spindly legs dangling off the couch, Edith dressing before anyone was up so we wouldn't be embarrassed by the sight of her in her pajamas. The Edith one. But she'd said before that she didn't do well in cold weather and that her stint at Cambridge had been a spiritual test. A very expensive spiritual test, she'd said.

"Thanks," I told Mam. "I'll pass it on. Listen, I need to go soon."

"Tom's here. Will I put him on?"

When she did, he sounded tired.

"How's things?" he said.

"Grand. Mam says you're a banker now."

"Fuck off. It's just Bank of Ireland."

"What do you do?"

"Piss-all, but then I stay late so it looks like I've been working."

"That's face time for you," I said, in a tone implying I'd come across the term in my natural environment and hadn't just learned it from Julian. "Hope it gets better."

There was a girl at work, Tom told me, but it wasn't a thing yet. They were still seeing. I didn't ask what they were still seeing about. He inquired about Julian with a degree of skepticism I found brazen in a younger sibling. I told him about Edith—not that she was my girlfriend, but that she was an important person in my life and I'd like him to meet her. He said she sounded nicer than Julian.

"I miss you," I said. "I need to go now."

"Yeah, sure. Keep me posted on Edith."

Sometimes the children had questions about my life. The younger ones wanted to know if I slept in the school, and if Ireland was the same as England. (Julian's banker friends had often seemed just as confused on this point.) The older ones asked if I had children of my own. I found this question horrifying, but knew that around ten percent of my salary was for projecting a nurturing aura, so I just smiled and said no. When they asked about men, I remembered that many of their parents would not want me teaching them if they knew about Edith. Probably some of them were old enough that they themselves would not want me as a teacher. I wouldn't want me as a teacher either, but not because I had a girlfriend.

33

Edith turned twenty-three on July 5. I used Julian's card to buy her a pair of quilted leather gloves. I wrote claiming they were for me and asked whether I should get them in black or cognac. He replied: "I can't believe you think I'd have an opinion on this." Then, five minutes later: "Cognac."

That night Edith took me along to a group dinner on Connaught Road. Her friends were all our age and mostly women. Cyril Kwok and Tony Ng arrived together and gave Edith a joint present. She'd mentioned before that some Hong Kong parents were more liberal than hers.

I wondered if anyone there knew that she and I were dating.

The restaurant had exposed red brickwork and clipboarded menus that called every item "artisan," "percolated," or "deconstructed." They'd got the head count wrong. Edith arranged for another table to be gerrymandered over to the end of ours, then through brisk intimation showed each of us where to sit. She was a spry conversationalist and used tailored strategies for drawing everyone out. Whatever I said, I felt people were only listening because I was responding to a question Edith had asked. She poured everyone water.

"You got a man first," I told Tony. Edith had put me beside him.

"Men are easy," he said. "Women are hard."

I thought I saw him smile.

The food came on slates, with condiments in clay espresso cups. Many of the faces were familiar from Edith's Instagram—which I could tell her later, but still, obviously, had to hide from the people themselves. They were all Hongkongers. Most had been at boarding school with Edith and had stayed in the UK for university, while others had gone to the US or returned home. They had the kind of brisk English accents that made my mother nervous.

Tony and I got talking to Clara, who taught yoga at a studio near the International Finance Centre. It was a good location. The bankers paid a premium for convenience and if anyone was understocked on the zen front, it was Hong Kong financiers.

"Ava," Tony said, "does it weird you out doing the neocolonial TEFL thing?"

"Yes," I said. "But no one else will hire me."

"I'll find you something," he said.

I shared Edith's assessment of Tony's proficiency at pretending not to be rich.

"There's nothing for me here," I said. "I'm a pointless white person."

"You're all pointless," Tony said amicably. "But I like you."

I excused myself after dessert when they ordered more drinks. I worried it might hurt Edith, but decided it would embarrass her more if I stayed and didn't contribute to discussions which all seemed to come back to people everyone else knew and I didn't.

I'd just gone to bed when she called saying she needed me to come and pay the bill.

"What?" I said. "At the restaurant?"

"No, TST. We went drinking. I left my cards at home because I thought if I took out five hundred, I'd only spend five hundred."

"How much is it?"

"I told you, I went drinking. And Holly can only pay half."

"Edith," I said, "where are you? How much is it?"

"This bar in LKF."

"You said you were in TST."

"LKF."

"Which bar?"

"I'll fucking, I'll show you on Maps."

"That won't work, Edith, because I'm not there beside you."

"I'll send a screenshot."

The bar was at the top of D'Aguilar Street. I took Julian's card, grateful he hadn't specified whose folly it was meant to cover. When I reached Edith, the friend had bailed, too, having left enough money to pay half the bill. I felt she probably could have covered the whole thing and hoped someone would make her leave her bed unnecessarily in the near future. Edith's curls were flat. One of her dress straps had slipped. It was the drunkest I'd seen her in four months of knowing her. On the walls, neon lights spelled out sound bites in uppercase: THE CHILD IS THE FATHER OF MAN; SILENCE IS MORE MUSICAL THAN ANY SONG.

Edith saw the name on the AmEx and told me to tell Julian she said thanks.

"He doesn't need to know," I said. "I'll say I was out with a male friend and he thought it meant something it didn't, so I paid for the drinks to clear it up."

"Or you can just tell him."

"No need."

"Does Julian mind when you take his money?" She seemed unconcerned that this might be a procacious question coming from someone who couldn't currently support their own head without the aid of both hands. "I mean," she said, "you're just flatmates."

"Actually, he's worried I'm not interested enough in it." This wasn't necessarily something I'd observed in him, but could plausibly have been true and was interesting to narrate to a third party. "He doesn't want anyone to like him just for him," I said. "He wouldn't know what to do with the information."

I wondered why I'd said that. I wasn't drunk.

We hailed a cab. Edith tried to talk to the driver, who ignored her Cantonese. "Mainlander," she said, rolling her eyes, and she negotiated our journey up Mid-Levels in what I assumed was Mandarin. I was afraid to ask if she considered her father a different kind of mainlander. Outside Julian's apartment block, Edith removed her heels and asked if I could take one for her. I wasn't sure how she could carry a single heel but not two, but felt it would be unproductive to question this. The complex was virtually empty. Edith complained that the cement hurt her feet, so we rested for a while on a stretch of grass in the courtyard.

"It's not fair," Edith said. "I love you so much and you don't want to stay in Hong Kong."

"I do. I'm always telling you I like it here."

"And I always say everything first. I asked if you'd be my girlfriend a couple of weeks back, and now I said I love you first and you didn't even acknowledge it."

"Thanks, Edith. Thanks for saying I love you. I love you, too."

And I meant it. This surprised me: I could never have been seeing someone for so short a time in Dublin and sincerely say I loved them. But there was room to feel it here.

"Good," Edith said.

"How often do you get this drunk?"

"You're obsessed with Julian," she said.

I'd had that exact thought before, in those precise words, and wondered if I'd ever told her. I said nothing.

"You're always asking what he'd think of everything," she continued. "You clearly have no interest in arranging things so it wouldn't be a problem if he stopped paying your rent. Which, why would he do that? He sounds like a rich freak, and you know he'll get bored of you sooner or later, because rich freaks are themselves boring people. It's only their money that's depraved." She spoke quickly and without looking at me very much, like she had said all this to herself before in front of a mirror. "And he gives you money. Why? Who leaves literally an AmEx for their flatmate? And why would he tell you not to have people around? I don't think you're interested in having a nice life. Which is arrogant, really, because you expect other people to help you maintain an existence that you yourself can't work up any enthusiasm over. Don't take this personally, by the way. I'm just observing."

"You're hammered," I said. "I do love you, though."

"My family are disappointed in me. They try to hide it, but I can tell."

Up in the apartment, I made Edith brush her teeth. She said she wanted to wear a bathrobe. Mine was in the wash, so I loaned her Julian's, which hung like a ballgown on her five-foot frame. A bluish bruise was surfacing on her thigh. She thanked me for paying her bill. I said I actually quite liked the idea of Julian seeing the tab and thinking I was having fun without him. Then Edith said she loved me again and I repeated it back to her, thinking about how some people were squeamish about wearing others' dressing gowns, but to some it was just like borrowing a coat.

We sat on the couch and she leaned on me. "Your family aren't disappointed in you," I said. "No one's disappointed in you. You're an incredible person."

"Thank you," she said.

I had no authority to say that about her family. I'd only met Mrs. Zhang, and didn't know what their internal dynamic was like. Still, Edith looked pleased. She nestled closer into me. I felt like abandoning everything else I did to try to be happy, and just spending the rest of my life finding things Edith needed to be told, and telling her.

34

Next day at work I had a cough that cut off all my sentences. Joan gave me a mint-green face mask. I said I didn't need one and she told me that if parents saw me coughing without it, they'd worry I'd infect their kid. At lunch I googled and discovered the mask was likelier, if anything, to breed germs by trapping hot air. This WebMD lore did not interest Joan. "Wear the mask," she said. I considered asking for sick leave since I was sick, but could tell she was in no mood for my funny jokes.

The twelve-year-olds were on the perfect aspect, God love them. They had just got to grips with the past tense, and the continuous would be next—if they survived. Present perfect if it's continued up until now, e.g. "They've been together." Present perfect continuous if it's been continuing, e.g. "They've been fucking." Past perfect if it: (a) continued up to a time in the past, e.g. "They had been living together," or: (b) was important in the past, e.g. "I had thought I loved him until I met her." There was more, but my windpipe filibustered it.

Eunice Fong said: "Miss, are you sick?"

I wasn't sure if I was allowed to say yes.

Dublin had its own take on the perfect aspect. I didn't know what to call it, but when you were "after" doing something, it meant you'd just done it but didn't expect the hearer to know. "I've just fallen in love": we thought it might happen and it has. "I'm after falling in love": look, I didn't think there was a heart in this piece-of-shit chest compartment either, but here we are. "Only after" was "just after" plus exasperation: mud on a carpet you're only after hoovering, losing someone you're only after finding.

Julian and his friends were "after" things meaning they sought them. They were after bonuses, after clients, always eating the dust of what they wanted. "After" never meant looking back on what they'd done. My sympathies were limited, given who they were, but I thought it might explain why they weren't happy people.

Ollie from Melbourne had left Hong Kong without notice to avoid paying income tax. TEFL teachers often did that. His replacement, Derek, was from Limerick. At a staff meeting to welcome him, Joan helpfully informed us that we were both Irish. Madison shared that she was from Dublin, Erath County, TX.

"'TX'?" said Derek.

Joan said: "She's American."

"It's weird how all the Irish leave Ireland," Madison said. "There's so much green. And you guys have the cutest accents. I've got this picture—hold up, let me find it—just chilling with Molly Malone. She wheeled her wheelbarrow . . . And here's me hitting up the Guinness Storehouse. 'A big bag of the cans with lads.' I'm such an alcoholic. Maybe I'm secretly Irish. And don't you have a gay president now? I can't believe I even left and I was there three days. What the heck have the Irish got against Ireland?"

I said: "You know we can't get abortions?"

I did not always feel I was Madison's favorite Irish person.

———

I loved Edith so much it seemed only sensible to worry about losing her. You could hardly stake that much in someone and not think every now and then of what you'd do without them. I analyzed the contingencies and concluded: nothing. On the couch or in my bed, I measured various scenarios in which Edith left me and decided my ensuing strategy would be: none. Up and down the escalator, pacing my clammy classroom: if she ended it, I would end, too. Sometimes this seemed fine and normal, and sometimes it made me grip whatever I was holding until my fingers hurt. When that happened I messaged Julian. Edith did not exist in the space I shared with him, which let me compose myself again. I wrote: everyone has too many feelings. it's embarrassing. He agreed. Inside my quarantined dynamic with him, I was safe. He'd made me unhappy, but I'd be in a far deeper gradation of misery if Edith ever abandoned me. She gave me concomitant highs. Sometimes felt I was hiding from those, too, when I talked to Julian.

35

Li Hongzhang, a Chinese general of the late Qing dynasty, claimed not to understand why Europeans worshipped Christ. He didn't see how anyone could get behind a savior whose own life had been such a bust he'd ended up crucified, a painful death and a degrading punishment besides.

Miles told me the story. Later I related it to Julian on the phone.

"He had a point, old Hongzhang," Julian said. "I doubt you'd catch Warren Buffett nailed to a cross."

"Is there anything you'd die for?" I said.

"I don't see what good that would do. Unless you're of the persuasion that lining all the bankers up against the wall would automatically make the world a better place, which you may well be."

"So what should Jesus have done?" I said. "Since getting crucified is beta carry-on."

"Ideally, he'd have founded a start-up."

During the call I made herbal tea. The mug was initially too hot to hold. It was a long call. I knew because slowly I could touch more of my skin against the ceramic. I thought: this is an efficient way of tracking my personal correspondence.

"By the way," I said, "I'm not fucking you when you're back."

"You really have been working on yourself," he said.

If Edith were there, I would have struggled to explain why we were laughing. I'd say: it's amusing when I tell Julian I might stop having sex with him, because then I'd have to live somewhere else and he knows I can't—and it's hysterical when he implies that me fucking him is a form of self-harm, because he's right. There would in any case be more pressing issues if I ever had to explain me and Julian to Edith.

The following night, he messaged about Kat.

Saw her at a party. Mostly fine. We talked about May's EU citizenship guarantee. She has this friend Izzy, and she (Izzy) said something about me "showing my face" here. Don't know if Kat agrees. Talk soon. J.

I read it in the queue at the Caine Road Starbucks. Experimentally, I typed:

i feel like you take me for granted, and particularly take that i'll still be here when you get back for granted, which is not unamusing when (a) i'm still not entirely sure you're not the guy in american psycho, (b) my girlfriend is i. a literal goddess and ii. almost certainly not that guy, and (c) i admittedly can't quite stop talking to you but i'm pretty sure it's just i'm so fucked up that i need a break from having feelings.

When it came to my turn to order coffee, I deleted the draft with an air of now having real business to attend to.

━━

I told Miles about Julian's take on the Li Hongzhang anecdote and he said it was the same reception Julian had given the tale when Miles had first told him it. Clearly Julian had feigned the same interest a parent would when their kid told them something they already knew—or had forgotten the story since Miles last told it, in which case his reactions were entirely predictable since he'd had the same one twice.

We sat on the roof terrace above Miles's apartment. He shared it with the building's other occupants, but today it was empty.

"I do appreciate your coming to see me," said Miles. "Have more wine. I've had a bit of a head start on you."

I wondered if most people's relationships with their fathers more closely resembled mine with my dad, or mine with Miles. My entire verbal contact with Dad since moving to Hong Kong had been strings of "How are you getting on?"—"Very good, very good, and how's work?"—"Very good, very good, and is it hot?" and then back over to Mam. We couldn't discuss politics because he'd say something awful about travelers or trans people and Mam would look at me like: don't be hassling him. The only thing we had in common was DNA, which gave us limited mileage conversationally.

"I wanted to ask you about Julian," he said. "How do you think he's getting on in London?"

"Fine, I think. He likes his job."

"I'll never understand him."

"Me neither," I said. "He was asking after you."

Julian had probably asked Miles about me, too. I wondered what Miles might have told him. There surely wasn't much he could say except that I was doing fine, and it would, I reflected, be unreasonable of Julian to extrapolate from this that I now had a girlfriend called Edith. Lots of people were doing fine and had no such girlfriend.

Miles said they planned to go to church some Sunday when Julian returned and I was welcome to join. They were Anglican, Miles said. My childhood impression was that Protestants sang a lot and were either more or less literal about wafers, depending how you saw it. Julian and Miles both had thick necks and voices whose timbre suggested a certain vim of throat. They'd be an asset come hymn-time.

I told Miles about mass in Ireland. My parents didn't believe in God and were Catholic to boot (I explained this wasn't contradictory, and was in fact the case for most Irish people), but Mam had made me go to the important services because if you didn't you'd never be Mary in the nativity play. I was never Mary anyway. I fidgeted too much, and the mother of God surely kept her hands still or gainfully occupied, not twiddling her ponytail.

Clearly I had some potential as an actress, or I couldn't simultaneously be Edith's girlfriend and Julian's whatever-the-hell-I-was. Edith's girlfriend was honest about her feelings. Julian's whatever-the-hell-she-was did whatever the hell she did. It was like the riddle with two doors and two guards, one who told the truth and the other who lied. And I had a privilege rarely afforded to stage professionals: I could choose which was a character, and which the real me. Could choose, as in no one else would choose for me—and couldn't choose, as in couldn't.

36

"We need to do something about the apartment," Edith said in late July.

She began by leaving freesias and tulips in the hall with a note: "put them in water or they'll die." I'd given her what I thought of as the spare key, though it was really Julian's. I wondered if Edith had taken this as a hint that I wanted her to reverse-burgle me with van der Bloom's summer selection. I had no idea how real couples worked.

I put the bouquet in a vase I'd found in the cupboard, coated in dust so thick it felt like silt. Later I rang Edith. "I put them in water," I said. "They're still dying."

Next evening the flowers were gone and there were new ones I didn't recognize. The tag said: "Tango Leucospermum, Kangaroo Paws, Scabiosa Pods, Eucalyptus, and in-season assortment." I typed a message to Edith asking what the point was of being a banker's moll if a year into it I was this unfamiliar with bouquets, then remembered sending it would be—probably—the worst idea ever.

I was a horrible person. I was living in one person's flat, fucking someone else without telling them, and regretted my behavior primarily on the grounds that it meant I couldn't mock the first person with the second. But I had a mythologically beautiful girlfriend and a nice apartment to share with her. It seemed ungrateful to say anything that might reverse my luck.

"I'm not keeping you in van der Blooms forever," Edith said. I'd complained the new flowers were dying, too.

"Come on, big spender," I said.

"Fine," she said. "Take the AmEx."

Like cross-pollination, our clothes went back and forth, her dresses in my wardrobe and my jumpers in hers. I saw her loafers in the hall and thought that if Julian saw them, the jig would be up. Then I remembered he'd think they were mine.

Really it all could be. Anything on his credit card might be something I was buying for myself. If his friends saw us together, it would be harder to persuade them we were fucking than we weren't. I almost wished I were still in contact with Victoria so I could say: I have found a novel solution to the administrative challenges of cheating. But I hadn't seen her in over two months now, and Julian had been gone nearly six.

On the last day of July, I was in bed, willing myself to sleep, not sleeping, refreshing things on my phone, when a message came.

> Just to let you know, work sending me back now. Flight next week. Logistics to sort so might be hard to reach. Let me know if anything you need. Thanks for minding flat. J.

I thought: someone needs to teach this man how to have a feeling, and how to write a message, and they also need to tell me what the fuck I do now.

37

AUGUST

August was too hot to walk outside. The day after I got Julian's message, I went alone to Pacific Place and walked a circuit past luxury outlets and American coffee shops. Outside Celine I mussed my hair to look like a disheveled rich girl, then went in and tried on a white blazer. The shoulder pads held themselves up as though my own dimensions were immaterial. The salesgirl seemed to feel that this also held for the rest of me. If I bought everything in the shop then she would have to accept that I was important—and really, I could spend my whole life proving that. I could probably get Julian to marry me if I said it was to satirize men who had wives, and then it would only be a matter of not taking too much money at once. He would certainly let me have enough for everyone to think I mattered.

Eight days till he returned.

My savings account had more than enough for a deposit now. I could move tomorrow if I wanted. I had nothing to fear from Julian coming back. At worst, he'd kick me out and I'd return to a life where one room cost me half my paycheck. That was how most people lived. It was fine.

On the ground floor I caught sight of myself in a big Zara window. How can you be that pale, I thought, and not be sick. It was all ridiculous. I ordered a flat white at a marble-tiled café, sat down, and drank it. The caffeine went through the appropriate channels. I thought: faster, please.

At first it seemed unlikely I could harm Edith or Julian. They were rich and smart, and I dented fricatives for a living, badly. But the trouble was that the more I followed this logic, the less I could see why they'd ever got involved with me. If they were mistaken enough about our relative status to let that happen, then it stood to reason that they might also, erroneously, be hurt that I'd been seeing someone else.

My thoughts over coffee were always quite interesting.

That evening I had pot noodles and wine for dinner. I watched a zombie film on Netflix, liked a post of Edith's on Instagram, and read one of Miles's PDFs. Finally I opened Julian's latest message.

We should have R&V for dinner when I'm back. Or take them out. Latter prob best. Been in touch with V & she says you've been ignoring her messages. All well? Not like you to not reply. Not like you to enjoy V's company either, but you need friends. Ask when they're free. Maybe a present for them. Just sth from M&S and I'll say I got it in London. & get Miles sth too. Don't write notes—I'll do that. Talk soon. J.

I decided to write one of my therapeutic drafts. I typed:

i'm fucking edith. i've told you who she is in previous fake messages, so i'm not sure if it's more consistent to pretend i'm sending this to the julian who's read them or if you're a new one now. it's all fake anyway. so: my girlfriend edith and i are in love. she doesn't know about you. also, it would not be ideal for me if you kicked me out of your apartment over this, so i don't know why i'm telling you. you say you don't have feelings, but if you do, i'm sorry.

I deleted it, went to the kitchen and drank more wine. The tap dripped. I'd meant to get it fixed, asked Julian who to call, remembered him sending me the landlord's number, but later couldn't find his message and didn't want to ask again for fear of seeming scatty.

When I came back, I reopened my laptop and saw that rather than "delete" I'd pressed "send." I laughed.

He didn't reply. At work I took toilet breaks to check my inbox and weathered Joan's dirty looks. On the MTR my data wavered, which forced me to go longer periods without refreshing. This made me think he surely would have messaged by the time it was my stop, but I'd climb up, get the signal back, and see he still hadn't. My throat felt tight and fraudulent. In that split preliterate second when I saw a new bolded message, my pulse jumped from me, then "TST tn? who's keen" in the teachers' group chat and it settled. I'd think: I am not keen on TST tonight, or ever, and I could reply to that effect in all of two seconds, but I won't because that would take effort and I am currently funneling all available resources—physical, mental, human— into not publicly screaming at how fucked I am.

Edith asked what was wrong. "You're like me lately," she said. "Checking and checking." I said if she did it then surely I could, too. "You can do anything," she said. "But I don't know why you'd want to be like me." I did want to be like her, but that also wasn't why I kept looking at my phone.

I could have told her about Julian at that point, but then there would be consequences, whereas if I put it off then I would not have to deal with them yet. This reasoning seemed sensible to me, and I wondered why anyone ever volunteered information.

Four days later, Julian responded.

A—bit of a strange message but I assume sent under the influence. It's fine. Not as if we're a thing, so do what you want. See you next week. J.

My abbreviation felt pointed. "A" implied both that he wasn't bothered typing two additional characters and that the indefinite article was quite enough for me. I wanted to reply: i agree that i am the least definite of any article.

38

That weekend I rang Tom. As we spoke, I stood on the balcony and watched children outrunning parents and put-upon cynophiles being walked by their Great Danes. We talked about Tom first. Things had gone downhill with his latest paramour. This gave him an appetite to hear about my love life, I suspected because it made him grateful not to have one.

"I can't believe you thought I hadn't guessed about Edith," he said.

"Was it obvious?"

"So what did you think would happen?"

"You mean, what did I think would happen if I didn't tell her?"

"Yeah."

"Well, broadly this," I said.

Tom said: "I struggle to think of you as the older one sometimes."

"I should tell her," I said.

Tom said he wasn't going to tell me what to do, but that I should think about who I'd choose. I mightn't have to, but if one of them said that, I needed to know what I'd say.

I told Tom I didn't know. I didn't want to weigh them up against each other.

"All right," he said, "don't compare them. But how do you feel when you're with them? Or, I mean, how do you act around them?"

That question was less daunting.

"I'm not nice to Julian," I said. "He doesn't love me and I feel like that means there's something wrong with me, so then I want to believe the problem is actually him. We laugh a lot, but I'm a horrible person when I'm with him. I want to make him feel as bad as I do."

It surprised me to learn that about myself, but there it was, out in the spitting air, echoed back to me thanks to the dodgy connection.

"That's not good," said Tom. "For either of you."

"It's not. He's not over his ex. I shouldn't hold that against him."

"And what about Edith? What are you like around her?"

"Kinder. More forgiving. And the sex is better."

"I didn't need to know that."

"Just giving you the facts."

"Cool. Well, like I said, I can't tell you what to do. How long until he's back?"

"Two days now."

"So one day to tell her."

"I probably won't," I said.

"That literally doesn't surprise me."

"I know. But it was good talking it through. Thanks, Tom." I didn't tell him that often. "I know it's not easy being straight with me."

"It's not. You punish people for it."

"I'd better go."

"Sure."

"Tom?"

"Yeah?"

"Thanks again. And thank Mam for me, too."

"You sound like you're off to the trenches."

I said: "You're not wrong."

Later that Sunday, Edith came over to the flat. We finally burned my Jo Malone candle. She had a red indent across her back where her bra dug in. I traced over the ridge and said I wondered what would happen if you wore a bra for a hundred consecutive hours, as in, would you get a scar. It was my last day left to tell her about Julian before he got back, and I was asking her about skincare. My behavior was fascinating.

"Have you heard bras cause cancer?" she said. "It's probably quackery, but I worry. There's a lower breast cancer rate in countries where fewer women wear bras. But it's hard to establish the cause because not wearing a bra correlates with not doing stuff like eating junk food."

I said: "Junk food causes cancer?"

"We don't know what causes cancer," she said. "Beyond drinking and smoking. But you already know they're bad."

"Yes," I said, "I do." Then: "By the way, Julian's back next week."

I was an idiot. I had no idea why I'd just said that. Probably it was that I'd told Tom I'd keep putting it off. Once I told someone I'd do something, I always did the opposite.

Her hair was a thick black brush on my pillow. It occurred to me that most beds did not come with a particular Edith, that actually most people had no Edith at all, and that those people had to sleep in those beds or other relevant furniture and pretend to be happy.

"Is he," she said.

I couldn't tell what she was thinking.

"I'm just after finding out," I said.

"And this thing," Edith said, pausing, not to decide what "this thing" meant but so the break would be long enough that she didn't have to put words on it, "this thing between you, it'll continue?"

"What do you mean?"

"You living with him."

"He's my flatmate, so."

"You don't pay rent," she said, in a just-observing voice like Julian's.

"It's complicated," I said.

"It's weird"—still seemingly just observing.

"You're into weird."

"Thanks for that, Ava, but I'm not sure this is the best time to tell me what I'm into."

"Look," I said, "it's between me and him."

"Exactly," Edith said.

She went out to the bathroom. I started to ask why she didn't just use the en suite, but she was already gone. I only knew the pictures on the wall meant London because he'd told me. The middle one was Tudor-fronted with carceral grids for windows. Tall English buildings looked like tall English prisons, and when you said that to an English person they thought you meant their prisons were lovely, too.

Edith came back. She stood in the doorway and held up a T-shirt she'd loaned me. I was about to say something, then saw she expected me to and couldn't.

Very quietly, she said: "Why was this in his room?"

"What?" I said.

"My T-shirt. It was on his bed."

"What were you doing there?"

"My question precisely."

"I can't believe you went into his room."

"Same."

"Edith."

"Why the fuck were you in there?"

"He's in London," I said. "I was watching movies in his bed."

"Why were you watching movies in his bed? And, Ava, please note that I'm a very intelligent person."

She held herself perfectly as I told her everything, meeting my eye as though it was too late to keep me honest, but she could at least remind me I wasn't. All was still, her jaw, her hands. Whenever I paused, she nodded. I felt she controlled the taps and I would speak as long as she wanted and stop at a twist.

Finally she signaled she'd heard enough by coming and sitting at the edge of the bed. She folded the T-shirt in half, then quarters, then handed me it once she'd got it down to the smallest possible dimensions.

"You haven't told me how you feel about him," she said.

"I thought I loved him," I said. "Then I met you."

"It's twisted as fuck that you're an actual kept woman," Edith said, "and I do wish to give that its proper billing as the thing that would bother me if something else weren't bothering me more. But something else is bothering me more."

I wanted her to say it all. I wanted there to be nothing left and to have my deficiencies out where I could see them.

"I can't tell what you feel for him," she said. "Clearly, he feels something, and I think you're desperate enough for his validation that you'll go back to him. I have many opinions about the nexus between monogamy and patriarchy, opinions which are available on request should they interest you, but also, I feel like his views are probably quite conventional. So then we can't be together. If that happens."

While I was demonstrably not the world's leading Edith-whisperer, I sensed now was not the best time to tell her Julian already knew and had claimed to be fine with it.

"Look, Edith," I said, "I'm not the sort of person he'd have feelings for."

"How do you mean?"

"He's got money and he's smarter than me. And taller."

"My understanding is that straight men like women to be smaller than them. Also, he doesn't want anything serious—and that's not me speculating, you've said it yourself. Then you come along and he just has to give you a room he wasn't using. I know the type. You meet them in law firms. He doesn't want a woman in his 'league.'"

I said it was comforting to know he was only with me because I was short, boring, and plain.

"I thought you said he wasn't with you," said Edith.

I told her she was right and that I'd only said that for oratorical effect.

"Whatever," she said. "I didn't know till now how much I love you, but apparently it's enough to listen to your bullshit about oratorical effect and he's taller than me so how can he fancy me, and of course it's normal to have sex with two people in the same bed and not tell either of them."

"It was always his bed," I said. I wanted to take her hand but didn't dare. "Mine was just you."

This logistical clarification assuaged her more than I'd thought it would.

"So will you keep fucking him when he gets back?" Edith said.

"No," I said. I realized when I heard it that it was a decision.

"You'll move out," she said.

"Yeah. But is it okay if I stay for a few weeks? Just until I find a place."

She looked like she had something cold in her mouth that was hurting her teeth.

"Also," I said, "you're wrong about Julian not being nice. He's nice."

"It says a lot about you that you think that proves you don't love him."

I couldn't look at her. It was too accurate.

"That's such a misogynist trope," I said. "Women not liking nice guys."

"Some people," Edith said, "fit a great many misogynist tropes into their personal lives."

PART III

EDITH AND JULIAN

39

SEPTEMBER

We took the ferry to Lamma Island. Edith wore a straw hat with a black band. Julian brought his laptop and tapped at emails. I sat in between and watched the foam curdling against the boat as it churned through the water.

"She must be out of her mind," Julian had said when I'd told him Edith wanted the three of us to do something together.

"You guys would get along."

"She can't really want to meet me."

One of the stranger things about Julian, though, was that he'd say no to something, then come back later and say: no problem. I couldn't force an about-face, but could reasonably expect it if I made sure not to mention the issue in the interim. "Do you still think we should hang out with Edith?" he'd said in the kitchen a few days later. At least I was still good at something.

First we went walking. Edith held a parasol. There was a lot of greenery, scrunches of shops, and seafood restaurants with white plastic tables. Ante-prandial fish swam their last in tight-packed tanks. I said: "Can we save one?" Julian seemed to decide I was addressing him and said: "No." Edith looked like she was speculating if this was a long-running joke between us. I wanted to tell her we'd never be that rude to her, but I really had no precedent to go by. We passed balconied houses spread out up the hill.

He'd arrived two weeks ago at the start of September. The night before he'd returned, I'd thrown out Edith's edits—the flowers, the framed paper samples. I went to meet him at the airport and when we got back, he took his shoes off in the hall and put them beside the heels I'd left earlier. I added the sandals I'd had on and saw that this combination, one pair of his and two of mine, looked a lot like something else. I made tea. "I've coffee either," I said. "We've coffee." Tea was fine, he said. The kettle clicked and hummed. I asked if I could stay until I found somewhere.

For our Lamma lunch, Julian had made a booking at a raw vegan café. Even when he wasn't enthused by something—be it uncooked plant-based cuisine or Edith's company—he wanted to be in charge of it. She told him the restaurant was nice, and he looked at her pityingly like she thought he'd built it by hand and he didn't want to disillusion her. I wondered if he'd thought Edith was vegan—it was the sort of thing he assumed about women. We ordered zucchini noodles and hot turmeric milk. The tables were tiny. We arranged our elbows carefully around the plates.

"Ava told me we're not allowed to talk about work," Julian said to Edith, "so I won't ask if you've advised my bank."

"I never said that," I told her. "Don't believe a word this one says about me."

Edith said: "Julian, Ava mentioned you went to Oxford?"

"For my sins, yes."

"I'm afraid I'm a tab."

"She told me," said Julian. "Don't worry, everyone makes bad choices."

I said: "Like the one Oxford made when they let you in."

"Does she do this to you, Edith?" said Julian.

"He loves when I roast him about Oxford," I told her. "It reminds him he went there."

After our raw lunch, we went walking again. Edith led. Her dress reminded me of hotel bedsheets: creased cotton, limb-indented. Physically, I found it confusing to be around both of them: my face kept wanting to make expressions, something I now realized I censored it from doing when I was with Julian. I thought they'd had the same sense of humor, but now they were together, I couldn't think of a single joke they'd both like.

Julian's phone rang when we were halfway back to the pier. "You don't mind, do you?" he said. I went ahead to walk with Edith. The Chinese banyans cast weeping shade. They grew figs—Edith had told me that before. I kept watching her but couldn't do too much of it at once.

"When are you moving out?" she said.

"Two weeks," I improvised.

"You can stay with us. My mum could improve you. Everyone she meets, she sees room for improvement."

We'd reached the shops. In Central the signs blocked the skyline like pop-ups, ten per lamppost, one per story of a twenty-floor building, but on Lamma there were gaps between them. Awnings shaded the walk. A shop with sliding doors and no English name stocked postcards and dried meat.

The morning before this outing, the sun had woken me early. I got water and paced while drinking it in the lounge. I cut up an apple and did not eat it, and observed red-lined heels beside Julian's shoes in the hall but did not care. Throughout inspecting the shoes I continued not caring, and on seeing they were a seven formed no dubiously feminist mental image of her big ugly feet. Then I went to my room and cried, which was sometimes something people did, and as I was crying I heard Victoria say she'd best be off.

"It's hard moving out," I told Edith.

"Practically, you mean?" she said.

I said: "I love you."

I loved her that moment, yes, but also because the morning I heard Victoria leave, I'd put on a cardigan Edith had thrown on the floor.

Like Edith, it smelled of soap. I remembered how she listened whenever I told her about Irish, and then I thought about the places where things lived in her bag. I was one such thing now, I was safe there, and no one but Edith could hurt me. So that when Julian asked later that day if we were still on for Lamma tomorrow, I'd said: all good, and meant it.

Edith stopped to take a picture of the two of us. I asked if it was for Instagram and she said no, it was just to have. I could see her browsing filters. As usual, I felt excited to feature on her feed, but anxious that I would look mismatched with everything else there. I knew her caption would remind the people she was out to that I was her girlfriend, but wouldn't give it away to anyone else. That was more than I ever did to advertise our relationship.

The pier was just ahead of us now. We saw the next ferry was due in ten minutes. Having finished his phone call, Julian caught up. Edith asked if either of us wanted chewing gum or water, and when we said no, she went to get some for herself.

"That was fun," I said to Julian once she'd left. "I thought you guys got on well."

He'd started on a cigarette and gestured at the packet to offer me one.

"I don't smoke," I said, "remember?"

"Sorry," he said.

We could see the ferry coming in now, chugging and ripple-making. The sky bled yellow into blue. It was early for a sunset. I told Julian this and he nodded. Then he cleared his throat.

"I'd better tell you before she gets back," he said. I followed his gaze and saw Edith leaving the shop.

"Tell me what?" I said.

"They rang just now. Sorry, just let me—" He stubbed out his cigarette and lit another.

"What's happened, Julian?"

He exhaled. "My dad's had a heart attack."

40

J ulian said they were properly referred to as acute myocardial infarctions. At first, he'd thought the textbook had misspelled "infractions," but it was a different word—infarctions. The first hour after it happened, "it" meaning "an acute myocardial infarction," was crucial in determining the outcome. The "outcome" Julian referred to was binary in nature.

"He has coronary artery disease," Julian said. "Sixty-three is young for it. The doctors say it's the booze and fags. That or genetic predisposition."

Julian lit a cigarette, then appeared to remember what he'd said about the factors that had compromised Miles's arteries. It didn't stop him smoking, but he was quiet.

When he'd finished, we went back into the hospital. I gestured towards the lift, but he wanted us to take the stairs.

"You're both making a tremendous fuss," Miles said. "I lived through Thatcher."

Julian buttoned and unbuttoned his shirtsleeves. "I phoned Mum," he said. "She's getting the next flight."

"It's kind of her to come and support you," said Miles.

"Dad."

"Aren't you needed at work?"

"They can live without me for a day."

"Goodness, you really must think I'm nearing expiry."

That night in the sitting room I saw Julian watch a video on his laptop. It showed a heart like a rubbery boxing glove. A black patch spread from one of the arteries. Then came the plaque buildup, artistically realized as yellow bumps. Julian learned that Miles should have chewed an aspirin. It would have lowered the risk of a blood clot.

I said, "Maybe you can tell him now."

"Thanks for the input," said Julian, "but I'm not sure I want to give my father advice for the next time his heart stops working. Not exactly blue-sky thinking, is it."

A few days later, the last of Miles's tests came back. Julian found them reassuring enough to go back to work, but his habits got weirder and more erratic. When he was hungry enough to remember about food, he'd have whatever required the fewest steps: dry cereal, bagel not even cut in two. Small things irked him.

"Why did you put my phone on the couch?" he said.

I said: "I thought it was mine until the screen came on."

"You should have put it back. I might have got a call."

"You would have heard it ringing."

"No, I wouldn't. It's in silent mode from the hospital. Why can't you leave things where you found them?"

Later he apologized. I told him he could be as cross with me as he wanted, and he replied: "Don't say that. I need you to be normal."

"I don't want to upset you," I said.

He said: "If I ever say the words 'It upsets me,' please have me shot."

Florence arrived three days after Miles was hospitalized. She stayed four nights. She knew Julian had a two-bedroom flat and didn't know I was living there, but he got her a hotel room on the pretext that he worked late and wouldn't want to wake her.

Miles could only have two visitors at a time, so I never met Florence. Julian said this was for the best. She didn't take to other women. I asked if he meant their being in his life or their existence full stop. He didn't respond.

After a few weeks, they released Miles with a full complement of medicine and a list of substances that could and couldn't enter his body. We visited him at his home. I asked Julian if he'd prefer to go alone, and he said absolutely not.

"I don't even say anything," I said. "I sit there and watch you guys talk."

"You keep us civil. He hasn't held me personally responsible for the global financial crisis even once since you came into our lives. And I've stopped comparing him to Stalin."

I acknowledged this was a benefit not to be discounted.

Mam said Granaunt Maggie needed a hip replacement. Again, Mam said. Maggie had a turbulent relationship with prosthetics. The first fake hip had damaged some of the remaining portion of Maggie's actual pelvis, so now she was getting another, and probably suing. You never knew with the solicitors.

I said my friend Edith did law, albeit in another jurisdiction, and offered to ask her about it. Mam said she sounded like a nice girl.

"This other friend of mine is having a hard time," I said. "His dad's just out of hospital."

It felt indiscreet to say the friend was the banker.

"The poor lad," said Mam. This was likely the first time anyone had ever referred to Julian as a "lad." "Would it be serious?"

"He's grand now. He had a heart attack, but he's in remission."

"God love him."

"Both of them," I said.

"Sure look."

Mam's dad died when I was six. Like any number of men in our family, he'd been an alcoholic. You had to be careful of that, Mam said. I couldn't tell if she meant men should be careful of drink or we should be careful of them. The funeral was in the big white turf-smelling house in Roscommon. I'd gone back twice a year since to see Nana, who lasted eight years more. George and Tom watched telly with her and I'd go to the sink to wash up. "You're as good," Nana said. "Bit of initiative." At college I had tentatively described this as an example of patriarchal conditioning, but in fact I'd felt superior doing jobs while the boys sat there like spuds.

I asked Mam what to do about Julian.

"You're as well not prying," Mam said. "Just be there for him."

She put me on to Dad. He said: "Grand stretch in the evenings now?" and I said there was. He said it was well for some.

"It is," I said.

I felt important because now I was the one who couldn't see Edith. She messaged asking to hang out, and I said I was busy. I meant that I wanted to be there for Julian when he got home, but I obviously couldn't tell her that. So she probably thought I was dynamic and sought-after in ways I was too busy to even explain to her. That, or she thought I needed to manage my time better.

—

After Miles had been in hospital for a week, Julian took me to the Marriott in Admiralty. It was the first time we'd been out together properly since his return earlier in September. In the elevator a mink-coated woman scanned his height as though unsure he needed so much of it, then my hemline in certainty that a great deal more was required.

He let me order for both of us and said, distractedly, that my hair looked quite nice. We discussed whether the word "quite" magnified or diminished a compliment. I sketched a cline on a napkin and put "quite" between "a little" and "very." It was nice being someone else's Edith. Julian drew his own and put it between "very" and "extremely"—in this context, he said. In others, I was quite right. I asked which "quite" he'd used just there and he said he wondered how he'd managed to miss me in London.

"I missed you, too," I said.

He said I'd been a good friend to him.

"I want to be now," I said.

The seats were upholstered in a range of fabrics, overlooked by paintings of cliffs. The women in the restaurant wore bright dresses as though to atone for the glum-suited men—we had to have him along, you see. Julian and I started inventing stories for the ones nearby. He took as married a couple I regarded as quite obviously having a secret liaison.

"At the Marriott?" Julian said.

I said: "Sorry, I forgot everyone occupies a social realm where they're bound to see someone they know at a five-star hotel."

I felt calm in a way I never had before he'd left. I had Edith to go on real dates with now, so I didn't need to worry about whether Julian and I were on one. We could just eat.

He told me London had changed: not for everyone, of course, but for him. Nothing but the Shard was tall anymore. The Tube was shabbier than before. At least in both countries the woman in the announcements was equally anxious that he please make way for alighting passengers. He wondered if she minded hearing her voice in stations. There was no amount of money he would accept to have his own broadcast to him when he was trying not to spill coffee on himself. He'd thought he didn't notice the Chinese characters every-where in Hong Kong, but found in London that the signs looked bare without them, though his Chinese reading comprehension was still, he said, below that of literally a toddler. And he took the opposite view to Middle England's, re: London: he was freaked out by how many white people there were.

"Keep a wide berth of Oxford, so," I said.

Afterwards, we took the tram from Admiralty to Pottinger Street, then the outdoor escalator. Signs, as always: Sunny Palms Sauna, Paris Hair Salon, Open Late SEX TOY SHOP (emphasis theirs). It seemed humorous that Julian could be standing to the right, looking like the rest of us, when we had stayed while he was gone.

I realized I walked ahead of him now. The first time he took me to lunch, he'd reached the MTR station escalator first, then let me go ahead so—I soon saw—the height difference wouldn't be magnified on the steps. It had made me nervous. If he thought of things like that, I'd wondered what other observations he'd make. Now twenty-three was shaping up to be the first year of my life where the idea of someone noticing me didn't fill me with abject horror. I supposed later was better than never.

Inside the flat I made chamomile tea. I said: "I know you probably don't want to talk about Miles, but I'm there if you do."

"Thanks, Ava," Julian said.

We sat on the couch and watched the news on his laptop. He said he was thinking of getting a real physical TV. I said: "Christ, you really are pushing thirty." Hong Kong's government had jailed three prominent pro-democracy student leaders. British McDonald's workers were striking over zero-hour contracts. ("How can you agree with me so much and not like Corbyn?" "I think really the difference stems from our feelings on whether it would be in the national interest to turn Britain into a gulag.")

Julian fiddled with his shirtsleeves and said: "Do we have a date for moving out?"

"Maybe in a couple of weeks."

"Right."

I drank some of my tea so I could go and top up the water.

"If that's okay," I said.

"Well," Julian said, "that's not much time to find somewhere."

"Places move quick here," I said. "And I could get an Airbnb if I had to."

"True. Well, just know there's no rush at my end if you need longer."

Then he got up and looked for his MacBook charger. He should really just buy another, he said. Buy one for each socket in the flat, still probably manage to lose them all.

"I'm sorry about the message," I said. I directed this comment to the cushion I was holding. "It was an accident."

"These things happen," he said, as though people routinely sent him rambling declarations of who they were fucking. This was not outside possibility. His friends were pretty weird.

"So, Victoria," I said. I didn't know if she'd been back since, but I hadn't noticed if she had.

"How did you—"

"I'm a very intelligent person."

"You don't mind?"

"No," I said. "I did, but if I've got someone—"

He laughed. "I hope no one holds me to my mistakes as much as all that."

It had never made sense to me that men thought women they'd had sex with would like to hear them be unkind about other women they'd had sex with. You would have to be a raging egomaniac, I thought, to think those men didn't also speak about you that way. The worst thing Julian had ever said about Kat was that she was "fine," and that was one of the reasons I trusted him. It wasn't my business to mind that he was now doing and saying things he wouldn't have previously, but it worried me.

I went to the window so he wouldn't have to look at me, and said: "Do you want me to stay until Miles is better?"

"The doctor said he'll be fine in a few weeks," Julian said.

With my fingers I brushed stray soil from a potted plant off the windowsill, then went to the bin and dusted it off my hands. The plant was a gift from Edith. She'd said I couldn't really feel safe living where nothing grew.

"I can stay," I said. "If it would help."

I expected him to say, "If you like," and that I'd need a good half hour to determine whether he could do without me. Women took care of men and let them pretend we didn't. I knew it was unfair to compare Julian to someone whose entire schooling hadn't told them crying was for women and poors, but I remembered Edith thanking me for how I'd handled Mrs. Zhang.

"Why are we drinking tea?" Julian said. "Let's have Pinot Noir."

"The Chambertin or the Clos de Vougeot?"

"That's not my accent."

"Okay, but which."

"Wait, fuck, we still have the Clos de Vougeot?" I saw him think: and she had us drinking tea.

My hand slipped when I poured so I filled his glass nearly to the top. I started saying sorry and Julian said there was nothing in the world less worthy of apology. I said he looked good, and he said that was surprising because the air pollution app I'd shown him had been as negative about London as it was about Hong Kong. I'd deleted it myself long ago. He said that was classic us. He had a point, though I couldn't decide what it was.

"Don't feel obliged," Julian said, "but I would appreciate it if you stayed."

"I will," I said. "I'm happy to."

"As friends. Till I know he's all right."

"Friends" could mean anything.

41

OCTOBER

It was October 1, National Day. Julian and I offered to spend it with Miles, but he laughed and said he had other plans already. Edith suggested we see the fireworks at Victoria Harbour. I wasn't sure what she was up to asking Julian along, too, but didn't probe her on it. He agreed to come.

Walking through the crowd, I thought of the conclusions people could draw from seeing us. A tall, fair man and two small, dark-haired women. Two whites, one Asian. We couldn't be related, but we were too different to be an obvious friend circle. Edith's clothes looked the most expensive, so perhaps we were her harried personal assistants. But why were we spending National Day together? Possibly Julian and I were Edith's friends from uni and had flown over from London for the week. We'd all gone to the same Oxford college, and Julian and I were married and visiting Edith following her return to Hong Kong so she could help us "dip into the culture." Could you spot a gay woman on sight? It was meant to be one of the superpowers attendant on liking women, but clearly I'd never had it.

Edith found a vantage point and told Julian to use his height to make space for us. "This is fantastic, isn't it," he said without raising his intonation. "A nice day out with my best girls." Edith shushed him and he laughed. "What," he said, "are you worried you won't hear the fireworks over me?"

I stood in the middle. Every time a firework burst, I squeezed Edith's hand. Julian craned his head forward like he wanted to appear more attentive than he was. He was conscious, I knew, that this wasn't a public holiday in London and that clients would expect responses within an hour. That was Edith's situation as well, but she'd done more on her phone on the way over, so her hourly window ended later. I wondered at first which thoughts they expelled to make room for such considerations. But this was unscientific. Actually, the brain grew new cells the more information you fed it. I didn't like that and was sorry I'd thought of it, because it meant they were getting smarter than me every day.

The billboards above us cracked out red, white, and gold. Kids shouted.

Afterwards I walked Edith to Sai Ying Pun station. There was a mural inside of people disenchanted with urban life. She said she'd had a nice time and liked Julian. Then she asked if there'd been any developments with finding a flat.

"I'm thinking mid-October," I said.

"You were thinking the end of September the last time I asked."

"His dad's had a heart attack."

"I know you want to be a good friend," said Edith, "but I don't think he'd ask this of any of his other friends."

"That's because his other friends are actual sociopaths."

"Still."

"Just a few more weeks."

"If you're sure," she said. We hugged and she went through the turnstile. I stayed until she was out of sight to see if she'd look back, but she didn't.

———

Proper school had started again for my students, though they'd continued coming to my classes all summer. The seven-year-olds were halfway through their module on sentence-level grammar now. A few days after the fireworks, I gave them a lesson on category nouns versus exact nouns. I hadn't heard of this distinction prior to opening the textbook. It transpired that a category noun was something like "vegetables," whereas exact nouns were "beetroot," "carrots," "broccoli." It was better to use exact nouns because this made your writing more precise and interesting.

The chapter gave a short explanation followed by an exercise: an A4 page divided into columns. On the left were various category nouns. On the right, you had to fill in at least three corresponding exact nouns. I told the kids they could use their Cantonese-to-English dictionaries.

Cynthia Mak asked what to say for "people." Did it mean "sister," "brother," "father," or "teacher," "doctor," "artist," or—

"They're all okay," I said.

"But if I put 'sister,' 'father,' 'brother' in 'people,' then what about here?" She pointed to the box marked "family."

"Okay, don't do those. Do 'teacher' or something."

"But what about here?"—signaling the "professions" row.

"Okay, something else for 'people.'"

"Happy people, sad people?"

"'Happy people' isn't an exact noun—it's an adjective plus a category noun."

"So what should I write?"

We looked at each other. It was indeed a challenge to describe people in a way not immediately related to how they earned money or their position in the family unit. I said: "How about 'friend,' 'boyfriend,' 'colleague'?"

"I don't want to write 'boyfriend.'"

I couldn't blame her for questioning the exercise. "Friend," "enemy," and "colleague" didn't seem like ways of narrowing down "people" in the way "apple" did for "fruit." An apple would still be a fruit if it didn't have any others in its vicinity, but you couldn't be someone's nemesis without their hanging around to complete the definition. The same issue cropped up with my earlier suggestions. "Family" was relational, and "profession" was created and given meaning by external structures. Admittedly "adult," "child," and "teenager" could stand on their own. But I still found it depressing that the way we specified ourselves—the way we made ourselves precise and interesting—was by pinpointing our developmental stage and likely distance from mortality. Fruit didn't have that problem.

———

Even a British man so very British and so very male as Julian surely had limits as to what he could pretend not to notice—on grounds auditory if not emotional—so Edith and I had been meeting in love hotels since his return a few weeks ago. The first one was on Lockhart Road in Wan Chai. She told me it was an hourly rental, which augured something tawdry, but it was upholstered and managed like any other budget joint. You just had to check out sooner. The sheets smelled clean, probably because they'd been sprayed to. We booked the whole evening so we could watch TV afterwards.

"I wish we could tell people," I said in an ad break.

"I like having a secret," Edith said.

"Would you like me if it wasn't a secret?"

"I don't know. We could try telling people and see if I'm still interested."

"Who should we tell?"

"My family aren't ready," she said. "I told Cyril and Tony about us. People from Cambridge know I'm a lesbian, but I don't think anyone else does. I suspect I'd be rumbled if I introduced them to my girlfriend."

She said things in that formal way when she was trying to be droll. It irked me sometimes, but I knew it was her way of coping with things. "So who else is there?" I said.

"Julian, I guess."

"But he already knows."

"It's a pity," said Edith. "It would have been so good if we'd told him together. He'd have been all, I'm so happy for you guys, I'm touched you're being open with me, isn't it great that we're sharing our feelings."

"That's a perfect Julian impression. I thought you actually were him for a second there." She didn't get that I was joking—or at any rate didn't laugh—so I added: "But I mean, you can tell him. Just maybe don't expect much of a reaction."

She wasn't looking at me. I couldn't tell if this was deliberate, but I didn't want to check her face because if I did and she didn't look back then I'd know she was doing it on purpose.

She said: "Do you think we'll ever tell people?"

"I wouldn't mind," I said.

"Telling people or not?"

"Either. It's up to you."

"But I want it to be up to you," Edith said. Then she laughed slightly. I felt this had a more credible softening effect when people did it by text.

"We don't need to talk about it right now," I said.

"That's such a Julian thing to say."

"What's he got to do with us?" I said.

"'We'll talk about it later,' and then you never do."

"I don't think I've ever told you that."

"What," said Edith, "do you think I've bugged your apartment?"

"I genuinely don't remember telling you that."

"Well, you did. You can believe me or not. And not to pester you, but—"

"I'm working on it."

"You'd better be."

42

The third week of October, Edith said we should do something socially productive. Julian brought the plastic bags. We walked along the beach and picked up rubbish. Julian complained that there was no point because if we came back tomorrow, people would have dumped more packaging on the shore. Edith asked if he'd heard the parable about the man flinging starfish into the sea. Julian said yes, and that he thought it was nonsense because the man should have tried to get to the root of the starfish crisis instead of sticking plasters on it. She asked if he meant by seizing the means of production, and his face said: why is it that everyone I know is a white-collar drone, a deranged Bolshevik, or in this case both.

We kept going till the shore was litter-free, then tied the bags and disposed of them. Julian said the recycling bins were just for show and it would all go to landfill, where it would probably do more damage than if we'd left it on the sand. Edith replied that if he had a better idea for how to spend the next socially productive Saturday, then he was welcome to plan our next tripartite field trip. He asked if she was quite sure there had to be a next one.

I left them to it. I had other things to think about.

They squabbled again about where to eat. Edith suggested a pizza place. Julian said London was cheaper and better for that sort of thing. Edith said we weren't in London, so she didn't see the relevance of that point. We wound up going for seafood at the Boathouse on Stanley Main Street, which neither of them had wanted, but which gave each the satisfaction of knowing that the other hadn't got their choice. The terrace overlooked the bay. Edith and Julian ordered a platter of crayfish, clams, and scallops. They struggled to fit it beside the fake peonies on the table. I got mushroom soup and didn't eat it.

The Boathouse waitress brought our bill. I asked Edith if there was a Cantonese phrase meaning "lie of omission." She said she couldn't think of a direct translation off the top of her head, but that there used to be a TV thriller series called *Lives of Omission* about the Hong Kong Police Force. It starred Michael Tse. They canceled it after thirty episodes.

Julian said: "Where do you find the time to watch so much shit TV?"

"I did most of my watching as a student," Edith said. "And it's actually quite good. It got loads of TVB nominations."

"What are they?"

"Never mind."

They seemed cordial, but they always did. I wondered what they were really thinking, and knew that in Edith's case, at least, those thoughts were probably hostile. I wished she could understand that Julian wasn't pulling me back into our old dynamic. Him needing me was strange and new. Also, his father had been ill. It seemed farcical that I even needed to explain to Edith why I couldn't abandon him now. On another level I knew I'd abused her trust and had broken it again since my first apology by staying with Julian past the initial deadline. Under this reading of events, which I did appreciate was probably the sane one, it was not much to ask that I stop living with the man I'd lied to her about fucking. But what sort of person packed their bags when their friend's dad was just out of hospital? This, I thought, was the trouble with being emotionally invested in two articulate people who both made their case well. (Julian hadn't exactly, but I made it to myself with the sort of analysis he would use.)

"What about you, Ava?" said Julian.

"He's asking what you think of Martin Schulz," Edith said. "The leader of the German Social Democrats? Julian likes him. I don't."

"Then I don't either," I said, and Julian congratulated Edith on having such a loyal stooge.

It had been sunny when we entered the restaurant, but when we left the hail shot down as though from a volley gun. We had one cheap umbrella, which looked wholly unequal to the task before it. They said I should hold it. Being the modal height, I'd keep it at the fairest altitude for the three of us.

43

E dith and I went to a bookstore café on Park Road in late October, the week after the beach trip. It had a red door and wicker ceiling lampshades. I brought over coffee and muffins, and Edith read aloud from an article in the *Scientific American*.

"'A recent study suggests that our ability to construct sentences may arise from procedural memory,'" she quoted. "'The same simple memory system that lets our dogs learn to sit on command.'"

Procedural memory stored skills like swimming and riding a bicycle, while declarative memory was for facts and memories. You formed phrases by mirroring patterns from sentences you'd heard in the past. That was why Edith said, "Do you have it?" where I might say, "Have you it on you?" We'd grown up hearing different versions of English. Consciously or otherwise, we reproduced them.

"But I don't say, 'Have you it on you?'" I said. "I say what you say. And you didn't grow up hearing British English. You said your accent was American until you went to boarding school."

"It's an example, Ava."

I was picking holes to keep Edith talking, but really I found the whole thing comforting. I was less responsible for what I said if I'd soaked it up from other people. If someone said something to hurt me, it wasn't because they meant to, but because they'd surrounded themselves with unkind people in the past. And if I wanted to be someone who dashed off barbed retorts and didn't betray investment in those around them, I just had to listen to the people I wanted to imitate. My brain would rattle off their sentences.

"But it's depressing," I said—again, mostly to hear Edith's response. "Our words don't mean anything."

"I don't think the selection of the content is procedural, just how we use grammar to express it."

Then she went to buy a book. She put it in the middle section of her bag when she got back. Her manner made it clear that she expected me to raise what we'd been avoiding.

"I'm worried about him," I said. "We drink wine and he tells me things. I don't think he has anyone else to talk to."

"What sort of things does he tell you?"

"He believes in God."

"Is it quite necessary for you to live with him so you can have theological debates?"

"We don't debate it," I said. Her face was impassive, so I kept mine that way, too. "I don't really care."

"I don't feel that's quite as compelling a counterpoint as you think it is." Calmly.

"Edith, you're being such a lawyer." I'd intended this to sound playful. It did not.

"Ava, you're being indecisive."

She was still calm, and I hated her for being able to keep it up longer than I could. Probably Edith did not feel things as strongly as I did. She was at an unfair advantage. Or she experienced the same intensity of emotion as I did, but her feelings were normal and appropriate, whereas mine were sick and misdirected.

"I'm not being indecisive," I said. "I love you." Which I did, or I wouldn't hate her. "But I'm not going to turn my back on everyone else. This is so like you. I'm here in this country where I have literally no one but you—I haven't seen my family in over a year—but that's not enough for you."

"First of all," Edith said, "it's disingenuous to take 'Please don't live with some guy you used to fuck' as 'Please cut off everyone in your life.'"

Her voice faltered for the first time. I was proud of myself for that.

"That's the practical outcome of what you're asking," I said.

"Let me finish. That's the first thing." She raised one finger, as though guiding us through an agenda. The twinning of this corporate gesture with her raised voice terrified me. "The second thing is, you're so full of shit about not having anyone." A second finger, to show we were on bullet point number two. "Your coworkers invite you out all the time and you never go. Weren't your old flatmates texting asking to catch up? And Victoria said you never reply to her messages."

"Victoria's not the best person to bring into this."

"I—whatever, I don't want to know."

"Hey, Edith," I said, "just by the way, whatever happened to your many opinions on the nexus between monogamy and patriarchy?"

Edith took a napkin and brushed crumbs into it. "I think my opinions on lying are more relevant here," she said.

"What do you mean?"

"If you really think there's nothing intrinsically wrong with fucking multiple people—and you're right, there isn't—then why did you lie to me?"

"You can't drag that up."

"I'm sorry if my feelings on being lied to are spilling over where you don't want them," said Edith, "but like my opinions on monogamy and patriarchy, they are many." She had given up enumerating the agenda with her hands now.

"You said you'd forgiven me," I said.

Edith swept the table again with another napkin, though there was now nothing for it to catch. She considered it, crumbled and empty, and then placed it with care in her empty coffee cup.

I looked around the shop. It was crowded with people who did not share my emotional state. The books were menacing. I hated them—the chalky smell, the blackboard feel.

Eventually Edith said: "When on earth did I say I'd forgiven you for lying?"

I said: "You said you wanted to meet him, and now you've met."

"Apologies if I'm being legalistic, but I don't think that means I forgive you."

"So you're going to hold it against me forever."

"No, Ava," she said, "I'm going to hold it against you until you do anything to show I'm one-tenth as important to you as you are to me."

"You have so much," I said. "You've got a big family and most of them are here. They all love you. Even Mrs. Zhang loves you. You earn twice, three times what I do at your job, and as far as I know they let you piss. You've got friends."

"We can return, if you want, to the fact that you push away anyone who wants to be friends with you."

"I didn't push you away."

"Didn't you?" said Edith. "I was always the one asking to hang out. I'd think: this is pathetic, and I'd wait to see if you'd ask me, and then—still thinking, mind you, that it was pathetic—I'd give up and ask. And you know so much more about me than I do about you. The truth is, you like Julian because he enables this perception you have of yourself as a detached person. Plenty of people are willing to offer you intimacy. That terrifies you. You prefer feeling like no one will ever love you."

"My friendship with Julian is none of your business."

"You make me feel like I'm not good enough for you."

"Edith," I said, "all you ever do is make me feel like I'm not good enough for you."

She picked up her small tidy bag with the book zipped inside, stacked plate on plate, and then put both our cups on the top one.

"Come and stay with my family," she said. "Come tonight."

"What?"

"There's a free bedroom. Mrs. Zhang likes you. We need a fourth person for mah-jongg. Pack your things and come."

"Is that a threat?"

"No," Edith said. "I'm breaking up with you if you don't, but for that to count as a threat, it would have to be something you're afraid of."

I said: "I'm breaking up with you anyway."

Edith laughed, took the plates to the counter, then walked out.

44

NOVEMBER

At the Caine Road Starbucks I typed sluggish fake apologies. I did it straight into the message app, at first because I thought this would force me to send it since Edith had seen me typing anyway. This didn't work, but I carried on because—with my signature mental clarity—I thought switching to notes would be bad luck. The first draft said: i'm sorry. Later versions elaborated. My "breaking up with you" had come out procedurally, I said. But Edith thought procedural memory only decreed how you said the thing, not its contents, so that wouldn't help.

The green-and-brown coffee-shop decor made me think of dying trees. I never saved what I'd written, but kept the template in my head for the next version. The basic format lodged itself so firmly in my mind through repetition that I almost began to feel my behavior made sense. Then I looked at the discarded blueberry muffin I shared my table with and remembered how things actually stood.

The earlier drafts were all versions of:

i don't know why i said that. i don't want to break up with you. but can you understand why i'm scared to move out? julian's apartment is my home. so i panicked & said something stupid i didn't mean. i

couldn't move when you left. i sat there and breathed in the dead
books. breathed is two syllables when i say it and only one when you
do. that could be important but maybe it isn't.

I spent weeks doing this. October turned to November, and still I
had no girlfriend. I wondered if I could get a poem out of that.

Because I'd typed the first-draft apology in the Caine Road Starbucks, I felt it would be bad luck to switch. The baristas came to recognize me, bringing the total number of Hong Kong coffee shops that
knew me to three. I didn't care. If they wanted to look at my greasy
hair and pen-stained jumpers and decide that this person was me,
they were welcome to. I stopped wearing lipstick and put on which-
ever clothes I found on the floor each morning, which in practice
probably meant I wore the same outfit every day.

when we were together i felt too much sometimes and i'd go and talk
to him to calm down. he doesn't make me as happy or as sad as you
do. that means i care less about him, but it also makes it hard to
leave him entirely. he's like the gulf stream. did you learn about the
gulf stream? it keeps ireland temperate.

The first time Julian asked what was wrong, I told him I was on
my period. He was so medically illiterate on the female body that
I stretched this alibi to cover the initial two weeks of the breakup.
Then I said things were difficult at home.

"In Ireland?" he said.

I said: "Where else would I mean?"

There was no one I could talk to. Tom wouldn't get it. Tony or
Cyril might, but I couldn't reach out to them when I only knew them
through Edith. We'd only hung out a few times and they'd tried to like
me for Edith's sake. And she'd have told them by now. They hated me.
I was a bad person who did not know how to love.

For the first time in ages, I went to LKF for drinks with the teachers at my center. From the rooftop, the lines of the city spread like sheet music. George Sand had loved Chopin and he died on her—"Careless," Edith had huffed. We'd listened to his mazurkas on my laptop with the lights off. The blue screen was a lighthouse standing sentry. Later, Edith said there was an app to make the colors warm at night. It helped you sleep. I tried it but disliked the orange tint.

The teachers made me act happy. "Come dance," said Madison from Texas.

I came/danced. A man asked my name. "Kitty," I said. He said it was a stripper name. I said: "Why did you say that?" He said it was a joke. I asked where the humor lay and he explained it was funny because I was not really a stripper. I claimed to feel sick, went to the toilets, and sat in a cubicle typing: i'm sorry, deleting it, typing, deleting.

———

"Who drew Mona Lisa?" asked one of the girls.

"Leonardo da Vinci," I said. No matter how dire everything else was, I could get immersed enough in their world that I was pleased with myself for knowing things like that. It wasn't just famous people either. I'd provide the verb for what you did with a knife ("cut") and I'd feel I'd been handed one of the good brains. This was why people became teachers, I thought. It wasn't to help people. It was to be the cleverest person in the room, always, or at least to have people sufficiently confident you'd be that they'd call it your job and pay you for doing it. Really, it was more impressive that my eight-year-olds knew Mona Lisa existed than it was that I knew who'd created her.

They told me they'd read on the news that Leonardo da Vinci belonged to a—"Cult," I supplied—and had left—"Symbols," I said—in the picture. I asked whether they meant he was in the Illuminati, tracing a triangle in the air with my index finger. They said maybe. Mona Lisa had small numbers and letters painted into her eyes. They were invisible from far away, but you could see them if you used a— "Magnifying glass."

"Miss, did you go to Paris?" said one of the boys. He meant "Have you been?" but I only misunderstood for a beat. I told him I "had" and hoped he'd deduce from this that he should have used the perfective aspect. The kids drew the Eiffel Tower on the whiteboard.

"Finish," Phillip Goh said. I reminded him to say a "t" at the end: "Finisht," or better yet, "I'm finisht." I ticked his answers mechanically. If all students were as good as Phillip, I thought, then I could soon be made redundant by AI. In a way, it helped my job security to ensure they kept making a certain number of mistakes. I wrote "Super! :)" at the bottom of the page, conscious that a computer could do this also.

Someone else said: "Miss, do you have a husband?"

———

The Edith drafts progressed from straightforward groveling to something wiry and confessional.

> i can't believe you think i'm detached. i have more feelings than literally the central nervous system. but that's not what you said, is it? you said i want to *think* i'm detached. look, that's true. people hated me in school. at college i didn't give them the opportunity. i felt like all of me was a secret. i know now it was just that i liked girls, but i thought i had to hide everything. i thought if i let anyone in, they'd find out what was broken about me. and then not only would they know, i'd know too.

I still didn't send the messages.

———

In mid-November Julian and I went to St. John's Cathedral with Miles. We walked up Garden Road towards the bells. The outside was plain as churches went. "RV," Victoria Regina, was carved on the tower. Inside it reminded me of the Catholic one in Dublin: cream walls, dark wood. Miles said one of the pews still bore the Royal Family crest. It had been reserved for their visits before the handover. I tried to imagine a life so constricted that everywhere you visited, it was preordained where you would park your arse. While it did the constitution a world of good to get one's weekly fill of the blessed poor, one couldn't risk sitting next to one. The latterly inheriting meek were well and good, but best kept at a distance where one couldn't smell them.

Later, Julian took me for lunch at Sorabol on Percival Street. He told me how to pronounce "jaengban guksu" and that the Korean writing system was a cross between an alphabet and a syllabary. I wanted him to come out faster and more fervently with his facts, was aware that this was tantamount to wishing he were someone else entirely, and knew exactly who that person was.

He lit a cigarette on the way out. "I take it you don't want to talk," he said, "about whatever it is."

"No," I said. "But thanks."

———

Edith hadn't opened my Instagram stories since our breakup a month ago. I knew that didn't necessarily mean she wasn't thinking about me, because I wasn't watching hers and I thought about her constantly, but she was busy and well liked and I wasn't. I discovered a trick where I could tap the story next to Edith's, then swipe halfway to the right and see some of what she'd posted without Instagram registering that I'd viewed it. Once I accidentally flicked all the way over. I nearly dropped my phone. The content itself did not warrant this anxiety: it was a picture of one of her chai lattes in Sheung Wan. I screenshotted it anyway because if Edith was going to see I'd been stalking her then I wanted something to keep from the experience.

I wished someone would hurt me and Edith in a way that connected us, like robbing both our life savings or posting the pictures we'd sent each other online. Then we'd hate the person who'd defrauded or revenge porned us or whatever and we'd like each other again without my having to be brave. I didn't really want that to happen, obviously. I just felt anything would be easier than apologizing. I'd been terrified of Edith when she threatened to end it. I couldn't say sorry now or I'd feel that fear again.

i broke up with you because you threatened to break up with me. i felt your power and wanted to feel my own. i did. it worked. i hate it.

45

I'd survived my first Hong Kong winter without Edith. The second was proving challenging. Julian's bankerish perception of what counted as a trek had rubbed off on me so much that I now spent my life in four places: the apartment, the TEFL school, Starbucks, 7-Eleven—all on the Island line. In the morning I melded with the commuting rank-file, walk-elevator-walk-train-walk, and looked for facts on my phone. I discovered Colombia also had outdoor escalators, that 7-Eleven was in seventeen countries, and that Starbucks had dipped into Hong Kong's shark-fin trade.

Teaching kept me busy. Sometimes I made it until lunch before starting another draft for Edith.

i liked women first. men came later. when i learned what love meant, it was liking girls. but when i learned what liking girls meant, it was an accusation. i think that's why it's hard for me to love. my first memories of love are bound up with my first memories of being hated. i know you've been through it too & it's not an excuse. but i wish i could talk to you about it.

In the staffroom I said I'd given out to Jessica Leung for bullying. The teachers told me "give out" wasn't standard English. Steve from Vancouver said it sounded like a euphemism. I said Irish English was many things, but a bowdlerizing force it was not. "Riding" was about the most literal way one could describe sex, for boring straight people anyway. In actual Irish, I said, you'd be ag bualadh craiceann: beating skin. In Dublin the shift was just the shift, but elsewhere it could mean considerably more than that. Madison from Texas made to say something. I interrupted her. I felt Edith had taught me much about stoppering morons, and that the morons were lucky we'd broken up before I'd honed this skill to the point of never letting them say anything.

I'd never used to talk about Ireland with my coworkers, or about sex, or anything interesting. I hadn't tried at all. I knew I was mediating my new efforts through Edith's imagined approval, though in fact she hated me and was right to.

i act blasé about my family but i have no idea how they'd take it. i thought moving to hong kong would help, but it's given me more to hide. tom is fine, and i think george & my parents voted yes for same-sex marriage, but so did the girls in 6th year who made up i'd shagged my best friend and she wouldn't speak to me bc they'd said that. do you know how much it hurt seeing their "YES EQUALITY 2015" profilers? the worst bit is they don't remember. they call themselves ~allies~ now. and maybe they are. but fuck.

My twelve-year-olds were on quantifier nouns: a tube of, a stack of, a stick of. Some words only went with some nouns, and there was, I gaily informed them, no logic to it whatsoever. They nodded. They didn't expect any. This was, after all, English.

They did their exercises. As they worked, I thought about Edith. She had once explained that Cantonese counted nearly everything with a unit word. She reminded me that this sometimes happened in English: you could have a piece of news, but not a loaf of news or a bottle of news, and you said "two pairs of pants" rather than "two pants." Then she told me to imagine most nouns were subject to such constrictions. "That's Cantonese," she'd said. "That's how it works in Cantonese."

She'd had me repeat phrases after her. Yat daahp bouji: a pile of newspapers. Go bat chin: a sum of money. Li peht laih: this patch of soil. I asked when she anticipated I would need to discuss this or any other patch of soil in the near future, and she said I never did anything practical with my life anyway, so there was no need to focus on quote-unquote handy phrases.

Another draft:

that thing you said about julian letting me think i'm detached is true. that's us. but there's a friction too. you said it's normal to feel something when there's history, but i don't think it's me still fancying him. there's a level of that, but nothing major. it's more that we can't talk to most people but can to each other. i'm 99% not sending you these bc i'm afraid to, but the other 1% feels like you want me to cut him out & i don't think i need to. "friction" is too sexy for what i mean. i'll choose a better word in the next draft. it's more . . . we're similar people.

That day back when we were speaking, I'd told Edith we did weird things with enumeration in Irish—that "two" could be "dhá" or "dó" or "a dó" or "beirt"—but that I wasn't sure if the grammar related to quantity classifiers or something else altogether. They didn't explain it in school. Edith said no one had ever explained Cantonese quantifiers either, but she understood them intuitively. "Yes," I said. "Well done, Miss Native Speaker. Congrats on not being robbed of your national language." She said that if I wanted to play colonial-oppression Olympics then by all means. I said I didn't want to play colonial-oppression Olympics. "That's wise," she said, "because white people generally lose."

i needed to be with julian before i could love you. i was scared the first time i had sex with him. i thought i'd be bad and he'd hate me. everything i did, i was scared. i was scared with you as well, but i was ready to be scared.

The evening before I went to meet Mrs. Zhang, I'd voiced my concern that I only used Edith's English name and asked if I was ignoring a plank of her personhood. She laughed and said her family used "Edith" more often than "Mei Ling" and that she identified more strongly with the former. She didn't say I was being condescending. She didn't need to. I wished I had her talent for making herself understood.

"Miss, is this good?"

I looked and saw that Anson Wu had circled "a kilo of books." They could certainly weigh that much, I thought, and more if they were Julian's, but the answer key didn't see it that way.

46

J ulian, Miles, and I went back to St. John's Cathedral the third
     Sunday of November. The sermon was on the final exam down
     the road. Before Jesus, we would be accountable for every-
thing: words, actions, thoughts. I looked at the royal pew and remem-
bered RV, Victoria Regina, on the bell tower. In 1841 Victoria wrote:
"Albert is so much amused at my having got the island of Hong Kong."
Edith had told me that, adding that she, too, would find it droll if the
Qing dynasty handed her a fiefdom.

That night Julian and I talked in the lounge. He said his ex-
girlfriend at Oxford had been like me. She'd hummed the Darth Va-
der theme when he told her he was applying for City internships. This
was fairly galling from someone whose hedge-fund father was bank-
rolling her to do unpaid ones at publishing houses, having secured
her said placements by ringing editors he'd met at Cambridge. The ex
was probably a better person now, he said. Everyone was terrible aged
twenty. I said: "Don't worry, at twenty-nine you've still got it."

"Wait," I added, "was this Charlie the anarchist?"

"No, Charlie was cool. This was Maddy."

"You and your left-wing flings."

"Kat's a Tory."

"So's Kate Bush," I said. "No one should name their daughter Katherine."

It would have been funnier if I'd said: let's not name our daughter Katherine, but I sensed Julian feared, as straight men often did, that I secretly wanted his babies.

I also avoided quips available to me about why he liked women whose animosity he could claim was ideological. Or why, if you followed the narrative late-twenties Blairites often held of having graduated into centrism, then he had matured to loving a Tory, lost her, and regressed to what I was quite sure he thought of as fucking a girl with campus opinions. Or why he hated himself for it, for reasons I did not understand him well enough to torture myself with in detail. Or why the obvious presence of those reasons nonetheless made it hard to look at him while he thought his private thoughts about how at least I knew not to pull the Rosa Luxemburg shit at parties while his friends looked down my dress and discussed me at what they felt was a volume loud enough that he'd hear and soft enough that I wouldn't, despite their standing in fact much closer to me, something they very much liked to do.

There was no more Clos de Vougeot, so we had Clos de la Roche. I said Ollie from Melbourne at work had told me Australians drank wine from a bag. It was called goon. Statisticians debated whether it was more responsible for Australia's birth rate or its death rate.

"By the way," I said, "I broke up with Edith."

"Fuck. You okay?"

"No."

"Want to talk about it?"

"No."

"Want more Pinot Noir?"

"No."

"Want goon?"

"You don't have goon."

"I have Pinot Noir."

As he poured, he told me it had a mineral palate, round tannins, and a long finish. I said it smelled like wine. He said "clos" just meant "vineyard" in French. Our vaunted Clos de Vougeot ("Your vaunted Clos de Vougeot," I said; "I don't vaunt vineyards") was founded by Cistercian monks. It and Clos de la Roche were among France's many appellations d'origine contrôlée, which made it illegal to use the name of the region without passing quality control.

"When Kat ended it," Julian said, as though this flowed naturally, "on the phone I'll add because importantly she wasn't in the room, I wanted to throw a bottle. I decided not to because it was my wine."

"So throwing other people's wine is a sensible response to heartbreak."

"Yes."

"How attached are you to the Merlot?"

"More attached than I am to you."

"That's not saying much," I said.

He agreed.

"So," I said, "can we have sex?"

"Now?"

"Yeah."

"Are you sure you wouldn't rather throw the Merlot?"

Somehow I wanted to have sex with him, and somehow I enjoyed it. It was probably the catharsis of accepting he'd never be my boyfriend. I said nothing satirical and accepted his compliments without caveating that I knew just because he liked my body didn't mean I could. It was like drinking something I'd been holding till it cooled, finding it still too hot, and gulping anyway because I'd been cold too long.

Since I felt confident now and hadn't the last time I'd had sex with him, there were theories one could form about who'd really helped me change.

And we still had to make it mean nothing afterwards, for different private reasons.

"Eight out of ten bad decision," I said.

"Nine, surely."

"Eight-point-five. And seven of that is me."

"Rob thinks you're a nine. Which goes to show lawyers can't add."

Julian had quietly swapped dreamy Seb for Rob since the party in February. I'd know to avoid Rob if the name changed again.

For a while we said nothing, and then he said he was often nervous around me. A year ago, I would have given the world to hear that. Now I barely noticed. I said what he wanted me to: that I'd never realized. He'd spent years at public school learning to feign confidence, he said, probably too much of it for some people's liking and certainly for some caustic Irish women presently in his bed's liking—but there were nerves.

I wanted to ask what made him nervous, but knew I would be doing so in the hope that he'd call me caustic again. He could just as plausibly say: you make me nervous because you often seem to genuinely loathe me. He could add: if you hate me so much then leave. Granted I am not someone anyone with a healthy attitude to intimacy would want to be with, but if I were, you wouldn't be here. You don't really want to try coke, and claiming you do is not a good look for a communist. Your interest in colonialism is at times morally serious and at times something you draw on when you're bored of hating me for being rich and male and you can't hate me for being white because you're white, too. When you find someone you can't hate for those reasons, like the cleaning lady, you pretend they don't exist. You're actually very good at getting what you want. You often get it without stating or even privately acknowledging that you want it, which lets you keep seeing yourself as someone who floats. Really you're more of a saltwater goddess.

(He would surely specify a classical deity, but it wasn't my fault I hadn't gone to Oxford.)

He could continue: the above is all true—not always, but often enough that it's part of your character. Beneath it, though, the main

reason you hate me, when you do, is that you're terrified of vulner-
ability. This is so both because others have been unkind to you in the
past, and because you don't like yourself and are sure anyone who
gets close will agree. That's what makes people afraid to offer you intimacy. They know you'll reject it. You broke up with the love of your
life because you saw how much power they had to hurt you.

This did not all seem to me precisely what Julian would say if I
asked why I made him nervous, but I thought it a fair stab.

"Who's the saltwater goddess?" I said.

"What?"

"In Greek mythology."

"Salacia. Roman, not Greek. Neptune's consort."

"I resent that you won't give me coke."

"Get your own," he said. "Jesus."

———

Edna Slattery was after painting the front door puce. She'd paid for
the paint, also the house, also the painter, so Mam did concede that
legally it was all aboveboard. But it was an unfortunate hue. You
couldn't trust the Slatterys in matters of decor. Jim had partial color
blindness, which everyone remembered except Edna. She'd ask his
opinion and he'd say it was grand because he didn't want to be forever
reminding the missus of his sundry visual impairments. Edna had
enough to be contending with. She'd tell you so herself. Where other
people had hobbies or interests, Edna Slattery had contentions. And
that, Mam said, was how puce doors happened.

"How's Dad?" I said.

"Doesn't like the door. He drives past it on the way to work."

"Poor Dad."

"And Auntie Kathleen's over next week," Mam said. "You don't
mind if we put her in your room?"

"It's more Tom's room now."

"I've already asked him."

"Tell Auntie Kathleen I was asking after her."

"She tried to send you a birthday card, but it got sent back to her. She rings saying I gave her the wrong address, and then she reads it out to me, and she's after writing: 'Mid-Levels, Hong Kong Island, Hong Kong, Korea.'"

"Where'd she get Korea from?"

"The same place she got Uncle Ger," Mam said.

We discussed when they'd call the abortion referendum. I hoped they'd give enough notice for me to get my flight cheap. I told Mam my British friend—she didn't know him—had refused to believe me when I said I had to fly back to vote. "That can't be how a country functions," he'd said, and then he'd spent half an hour researching the matter before coming back and explaining that I had to fly back to vote.

"That's Brits," Mam said.

She'd told me before about her year working in a London restaurant. She was nineteen. The Troubles were in the papers and the Brits asked whether she was from "their bit" or the "other bit," or else "Éire." (I felt Brits loved two things more than life itself: showing they knew foreign words, and avoiding having to say "Republic.") Camden was where London put the Irish then, Mam said. I said London put us everywhere now. Had to, on account of numbers.

"Mam," I said, "have you ever been afraid to say sorry?"

She said yes. If you weren't afraid then you probably weren't sorry.

"Then how do you say it?" I said.

Mam said: "You don't have to say everything. Just say as much as you're sure of."

I didn't ask what to say if you weren't sure of anything.

—————

I found it easier picturing myself with Edith now she was gone. We could live anywhere we wanted. No matter what our apartment was like, she'd find a way to make it nice. She would get animated about things, and tell me she loved me, and tell me she felt scared sometimes. I would start thinking along those lines, then realize that much of this wasn't an imagined future. It was things we had shared in the recent past. I'd broken up with someone who told me how they felt, and I'd gone back to someone who either did not tell me, or felt nothing.

47

There was a problem, Julian said, with the division of labor at the Starbucks on Caine Road. Of the quartet on duty, there would normally be two taking orders, a third making the drinks, and the fourth alternating between that task and running to the stockroom. But they'd chosen Sunday morning to induct a trainee barista, causing a double-edged dearth of labor. They only had three competent employees, and one of them was spending half their time on their own tasks and the other half mentoring the tyro.

It was the last week of November. It felt like he'd been back much longer than three months, and I wondered if time ever made sense in Hong Kong.

We slowly advanced up the queue. I said it was hilarious that the sign on the counter invited "New Partners" to apply, but that I worried my amusement reflected a belief that minimum-wage jobs didn't warrant grandiose titles.

"You never switch off, do you?" Julian said.

"You're the one analyzing their manpower shortage."

"It says a lot about us, what we think is worth delving into. I suppose it's like how Irish has all those different words for seaweed."

I didn't think the analogy made sense but was glad he'd remembered about the seaweed. He didn't normally retain much of what I told him about Irish.

Once we'd sat down, Julian told me his bank was moving him to Frankfurt.

I dropped my wallet. The coins clanged against the floor. "Leave it," I said, but he'd already picked them up. I took them and clutched them to cool my hands down, but the metal went lukewarm in my grip.

It was my turn to speak. I knew I should find a germane question. I said: "When are you leaving?"

"Mid-December," said Julian. "So three weeks from now."

I started stacking the Hong Kong dollars into piles of fifty. That probably wasn't five euro anymore. Currencies fluctuated. European politics played a role, of course.

"That's short notice," I said.

"They told me two months ago."

He stirred his coffee in punctilious circles, as though producing the whirlpool to a requested circumference.

I said: "Why didn't you tell me?"

"I thought, with Miles—they told me last September. I thought I'd decline it if—there was no point in telling anyone until I'd made up my mind."

I'd had more of my drink than Julian had of his, which meant it was again my job to make conversation.

"Are they giving you a raise?" I said.

"Yes."

This news was consoling. At least he wasn't abandoning me for the same money in a colder and less interesting country. I counted my stacks: 300 Hong Kong dollars in all. It was perhaps four hours' rent.

"I wanted to tell you in a neutral space," he said.

I wanted to tell him not to worry because the news wasn't important to me, but I couldn't find a natural way of putting it.

"Will you miss me?" I said.

I hoped my voice conveyed that I knew it made no sense to be sad simply because someone I'd just resumed having sex with was moving away.

"I need a cigarette," said Julian. "Could we come back to it later?"

"I'm ready," I said.

"You're quite important to me."

"'Quite'?"

"We've discussed this."

"Oh, the 'quite' thing."

"Yes. But if you prefer, you're 'very' important to me." (I could have done without the air quotes.) "You should visit."

That was the closest he'd get to telling me he didn't want me to come with him.

"You'd be too busy to see me," I said. "Especially if it's an important position."

He smiled like I'd just paid a small debt and thanking me would embarrass us both. "Anyway," he said, "I wanted to ask—could you keep checking in with Miles when I'm gone? I know he's doing better now, but he could use the company."

"Sure," I said.

My Hong Kong dollars were probably worth thirty euro, but maybe less now. The Hong Kong dollar was pegged to the US dollar, but that was only any use if you knew how the US dollar was doing, and their respective liquidities impacted their value on the forex market. Traders had names for currency pairs: euro, cable, gopher. Some of the coins were grubby and some were new, but they were interchangeable because money was fungible. I'd known that word generally, "fungible," but Julian had told me how economists used it. He'd told me lots of things.

I said: "Does Miles know you're leaving?"

"Yes, I told him a few weeks ago."

"Right." I said it the same way he always did.

"And by the way," Julian said, "we need to work out where you'll live."

"I'll manage," I said.

"Can you? I know you said your salary wasn't very high."

"It's good compared to locals'. They all live somewhere."

"With their parents, or else in coffin homes."

"It's really got nothing to do with you," I said. It wasn't what I'd planned to say, but my mouth was twitching like someone else controlled it. "Thanks for the guest room. That's all. We're done. Thanks."

We mutually agreed, through certain expressions, to pretend I wasn't about to cry. I thought that was generous of us.

"You brought me here so I couldn't react like this in front of every-one," I said.

"Clearly bringing you to Starbucks has been a very successful way of preventing your reacting like this."

"I didn't say it worked. I said that was what you were trying to do."

"That's not helpful, Ava."

"Why do I have to help you?"

"You don't have to help me. But it's probably in both our interests if you try to help with the situation."

"The situation between us? I don't think there's anything I can do to help with that."

I found it deeply unfair that he'd known what he was going to say before I knew the conversation would even happen. Logically, I knew this was not a valid complaint. You had to arrange things in your head before you said them aloud, and it was a fact of leaving that one person knew before the other did. Really my grievance was that he was in charge and not me. But I couldn't conscript him into staying with me, and anyway I didn't like him very much. And I didn't need him to tell me how much Hong Kong dollars were in euro. There was an app for that.

"I'm not talking to you," I told him.

"I can see that."

"No, but I'm not."

"Yes, evidently that's the case."

———

Some people wore not caring about money as a trait. I'd seen online that Julian's ex Charlie lived in Shoreditch and said without elaboration that she "created." If your work was an intransitive verb then that meant your trust fund subsidized it. Good for Charlie. Charming for Charlie to be a free spirit. For me, whatever paid rent was the decision. Sometimes there were multiple ways of paying rent, and then I got to pick between them. And sometimes there was no way.

I stood on Julian's balcony—while I still could. The clouds were bloated and the roads swelled with cars. My first Airbnb had been down along the other side of the port. I'd go back there, or somewhere similar. I'd felt different away from the cockroaches, but I saw now we had plenty in common—insects, climbers, cold inside. We thrived in hostile settings. There were places we did better, but nowhere could kill us. I hated them not because they were contaminants, but because they weren't. There were no pathogens they could spread that I didn't carry myself. Living uphill, away from them, I'd forgotten that. I'd thought my blood was hot.

———

That night in his bed, I told Julian we were now once again on speaking terms. He said he couldn't see the practical import of this pronouncement, given that I had continued to say words and acknowledge his responses throughout putatively not talking to him, but he appreciated the thought.

"But I don't think I was ever obsessed with you in a romantic way," I said, "or even in a sexual way."

"I was never obsessed with you, full stop."

"I thought we were past that."

"No, I'm serious. The only obsession I've got room for is my job."

"Right, because you're so busy and important."

"I thought we were past that, too," he said.

I wondered if he really wanted me to visit and if I could show up in Frankfurt with my suitcase and winter coat. He often said he didn't meet many people like me. But I didn't know if that meant there was necessarily a vacancy for them. He'd managed quite far without me, so it didn't make sense to assume he'd welcome me back in his life.

"Thanks for your time," I said.

"You, too. I haven't been this happy in quite a while."

"Jesus, you must have been a miserable fucker then."

He laughed. I could always make him laugh by saying something cynical in a thicker Dublin accent than I actually had.

Then I said a number of things. I said no one made me laugh as much as he did—which was nearly true enough to actually be true—and that I'd miss him. "And you say it's no big deal buying me things," I said, "but you think about money so much I assume it's not worthless to you. So it's nice of you to spend it on me. You've never been available to me, and I've spent a lot of time resenting that, but it's not like I've spliced myself open for you either. And you introduced me to Miles. You took me to see him in hospital. You've told me more about Kat than I've told you about my exes. And you were my first friend here."

"Thanks," he said, "I think. Most of that was quite complimentary."

He added that he'd thought of something he liked about me. "You're donnish," he said, "you're careful with language, you strain everything for its meaning, and you're not easily pleased with how other people put sentences together. Which is an interesting trait in someone who can't orally distinguish between 'three' and 'tree.' But when it comes to money, you've got no taste. And no squeamishness—about asking for it, discussing it, hoarding it. It's not often I meet someone who can handle it without flinching. Everyone is embarrassed. They feel compromised by even mentioning it. You're like that about other things, but not about money. When it comes to money, you're a little animal."

He added: "I was afraid to ask this earlier, but—come with me to Frankfurt."

I heard myself say yes.

48

DECEMBER

On my lunch break the next day, I started a new message to Edith. Within the logic of our imaginary correspondence, she deserved a phantom explanation.

there's nothing for me here. you, tony and cyril were the only people i belonged with. a little with miles, a little with the other teachers, but never completely. hong kong didn't make me happy, so i guess i'll try frankfurt with a banker who'd sell his mother to diversify his portfolio. that's not fair to say about julian. but none of this is fair. and that is okay for me to say, because when i say it's not fair i mean it's my fault.

I stopped typing. None of it concerned her now.

She'd once asked me how I made decisions. I said: poorly, what about you. She said she did pros–cons lists. "Usually weighted ones," she'd said, "because some pros will be more pro than other pros and some cons will be more con. And you need a column for implications."

"Implications?"

"Potentially important knock-on effects. Not a proper pro or con because you don't know for sure that it will happen—but likely enough to be worth considering. I favor the PMI table."

"What?"

"Pluses, minuses, implications."

On a napkin she'd sketched a mock PMI table for me. She was always drawing me things on napkins.

I'd asked how she'd decided on law. Edith said it was that or medicine, and with law you qualified sooner. "What about Cambridge?" I said, and she said her favorite teacher had gone there. The hardest decision she'd ever made was coming out at uni. Hong Kong international students talked. If anyone had wanted to ruin her life, they could have done so very easily by telling the Zhangs. But as Edith saw it, she would never be happy if she couldn't accept herself. She hadn't needed a PMI table to tell her that, but still recommended the exercise.

In three weeks' time, we'd be a continent apart.

———

For their second-to-last lesson before Christmas, my twelve-year-olds learned that British English speakers distinguished between "bring" and "take." "Bring" was for things that were going from "there" to "here," e.g. "I'll bring you some biscuits from the other room." "Take," however, was for things you were moving from "here" to "there," e.g. "Could you take the biscuits back to the other room?" The textbook said a speaker's ability to observe this distinction was a sure way to tell if they were native or non.

I had never heard of the bring/take rule. In Dublin you mostly said "bring." The "clearly unnatural," "incorrect" example sentences in the textbook looked fine to me: "I'll bring you to the airport tomorrow," "I'll bring my camera with me when I go to Spain on holiday." The textbook always referenced European travel destinations.

I practiced in my head to ensure I used the right verb with Julian when he flew off next week. "Don't forget to take your suitcase." "Will the taxi take you there on time?"

We'd fought about whether to fly business or economy. He said he'd buy my ticket to have someone to talk to in business. I said people would think I'd paid for it myself and I'd never get over the social embarrassment. Imagine, I said, being seen as the sort of person who'd pay that much money for literally a seat. Julian said no one would ever think I'd paid for business. I said why the fuck would he say that, he said he'd meant it by way of reassurance, and then the argument wasn't about tickets anymore. In the end it didn't matter, because work needed me to stay an extra week until the new teacher's visa came through. "That's not your problem," Julian said. I'd said no, it wasn't, but that I didn't mind.

"I still don't understand," Tammy Kwan said after I'd explained bring/take for the fourth time. Tammy Kwan had my sympathies.

———

There wasn't space for a proper PMI table on Edith's napkin. I went to MUJI in Hopewell Centre to buy paper. Near the stationery display, a small white aroma diffuser misted out cedarwood oil. I paid thirty Hong Kong dollars for a large recycled notebook with a red spine. The inside was blank. The woman at the till said she liked those ones because you could fill them however you wanted.

In my bedroom I opened the first page and wrote: "I'm sorry." My preteen students had introduced me to erasable pens. They liked them because no one would know you'd made a mistake. I rubbed out "I'm sorry," wrote "PMI table," underlined it with a ruler, also from MUJI, ran over it with a highlighter, also from MUJI, and then started.

———

Julian and I had planned to go to the beach on Sunday in mid-December, but the morning news said the shore had been affected by an oil spill coming from mainland waters. White bubbly clumps lined the sand like Styrofoam. Authorities were asking why it had taken China a day to notify Hong Kong of the ship collision which had caused the incident.

We had sex instead. I liked the authoritative clink of his belt when he undid it. Afterwards I curled up like a woodlouse and asked why he wanted me to come with him.

"I'm not sure," he said. "I suppose I enjoy your company."

"I don't even enjoy my company."

"No," he said, "you don't seem to."

"So are we friends again or what?"

"We're always friends," he said. "Christ."

"Don't take His name in vain."

"You don't believe in any of it."

"I feel Catholic guilt when we're fucking, but I'm not sure if fucking you is the source of guilt or the penance."

"'Better than Hail Marys.' Can I have that in writing?"

No matter how acerbic I was with Julian, it ultimately supported his view of himself as someone who could take it, and of me as doing it to please him. He enjoyed my sharpness primarily because it was an impressive thing to have on retainer.

"You blaspheme quite often actually," I said. "In bed, I mean. Babe."

"Get fucked."

He said "Get fucked" the smiling Irish way. When I first met him I'd consciously dialed back on it, also "Fuck off" and "You're a cunt," because the English for some reason did not find such statements affectionate. I wondered which other phrases he'd plucked. I felt like a bird he kept for quills. I remembered the times I'd lain on my stomach and he'd rubbed my back, and I thought, very sensibly: thief. He liked Irish English because he knew the most interesting words were ones he'd never say. I detested him violently, though I was well aware that the take where I stirred his inner poet was more flattering than the

likelier one that he'd got used to having me and I didn't give him much
trouble.

Which fairly described how I felt about him.

I started persuading myself that my behavior was different, then
realized I loved the idea that we were calmly exploiting each other
and would both go to hell when we died. If he went first, I'd get a bigger
advance on my memoir. Those heady days of pickpocketing bankers,
I'd write; and then I settled down with one in Richmond. He com-
muted, telling people it was because I liked green spaces, being Irish.
One could hardly plant a Celtic soul in Canary Wharf—or a soul of any
kind, he added, ironically of course. He married me, took a mistress,
and bought me an AGA. He denied this last was to atone for his indis-
cretions, because that would mean either of us had feelings. I often
dined with his mother.

Since Julian would never be my boyfriend, we'd never marry. The
fact that I could imagine a world where we did, but not one where we
were happy, was interesting.

I couldn't tell if he thought I wasn't good enough for him, if I was
ascribing to him that opinion so I could hate him, or something else
altogether. Maybe the something else was that he liked having money
and I liked being good at men. Neither of us liked much else about
ourselves. Julian knew he was small fry compared to his clients, and
I knew I was terrible at men if my methods made them happy and me
miserable. But we backed each other up. Both our egos thrived on him
being the richest man I'd ever been good at.

Not even that could be the worst thought. Nothing in words was
the worst thought. Something was inside me. Every time it hit my
consciousness, I redrafted it to something else.

But I'd go to Frankfurt. We suited. Julian was nicer now than he
had been a year ago, a positive trend which I hoped would continue. I
had no evidence that he wished to change and probably only thought
he did because I'd want to if I were him, which to some minds would
militate against our being together—but I didn't care.

I said: "Will we keep having sex in Frankfurt?"

"I don't know"—as much as to say: we might really be brains in jars for all we know.

"How can you be a theist about God and agnostic about whether we have sex?"

"Quite easily, Ava. I'd wager many people believe in God and don't have strong opinions on whether we should have sex."

"Some of them are pretty sure Edith and I shouldn't."

It came out before I'd finished forming the thought. We pretended I hadn't said it.

Two weeks left, then I'd be thousands of miles from her.

—

My PMI table took hours to do. For the weighting, I gave something very important a "3," moderately important a "2," and trivial a "1."

When I added the columns, it was a draw.

49

I packed Julian's shirts with just the bedside lamp on. They'd become so familiar that I took artistic pride in noting different cuts and textures. The COS one had a white rectangular label inside. He said he thought I liked that shirt more than he did.

"Just the label," I said. "It's a nice label. And the cotton smells fresh. What one are you wearing now?"

He couldn't remember. I put my hand on his neck and said let's have it off and see.

"You're acting strangely," he said.

I said: "I thought you liked that about me."

He said I was tired and that he'd finish packing himself. I stood up to go back to my room when he added: "There's something I should thank you for."

"What?"

"There used to be a picture of me and Kat on the mantelpiece. I took it out of the frame before you came over the first time."

"The Dublin picture is better," I said.

"Yes."

"I haven't seen the other one, but I know I'm right."

"You are."

"We can take it to Frankfurt."

"Thanks. Let's."

"I just printed it off the Internet."

"Ava."

"You're welcome," I said. "And thanks. Thanks for everything."

He opened the window, lit a cigarette, leaned out, and said: "Are you sure you want to come?"

I said: "Yes."

"I'm not sure you've thought about it properly."

"I'm an adult," I said.

In my room I tidied my drawers. I started with scarves: a few from markets, silk from Mam, and the one Edith gave me for my birthday. They were all too light for Frankfurt. Julian would buy me one, though the fun of that had deflated since I'd realized he did it to fill voids he'd never confide to me. I typed "how long does it" into the browser on my phone. Autofill offered: "take to get over someone." Algorithms learned quickly.

The room was cold. I tugged on a polo neck and my head got stuck in it. I laughed, then wondered if this was to check I still knew how to.

Not seeing the harm in drafting one last piece of autofiction, I opened a thread with Edith and tapped out:

i wish i'd been ready sooner, but i'm ready now. you've changed my life. i'll always remember that. i understand if you never want to speak to me again. it will break my heart if we can't be together. but you miss out on too much trying to keep it safe. julian can never hurt me as much as you did when you threatened to break up with me—not because he wouldn't, but because he can't. because there's nothing at stake. there is with you, and i'm done being a coward. it's hard to say how i feel but

I thought: I'm an adult.

I hit the back arrow and scrolled through other threads for

someone to talk to. Joan, last text: please stay behind tomorrow & help sort boxes. Tom, last text: free to call tomorrow?—sent by me, no response. Julian, last message: will you be home soon?—also sent by me, also no response.

Three dots flashed under Edith's name. She was typing.

My legs were dangling off the bed. I locked my knees to keep them still and laid the phone on my lap, inching it into place like a time bomb. I looked ahead at the framed London pictures, then back at my thighs, with finicky turns of my chin—up to buildings, down to dots.

Maybe she'd seen them under my name first.

Edith could have noticed me typing just now, or at any point before. Through all my screeds, all my work and reworking, she might have seen the animation.

Dot, dot, dot.

I knew Edith was typing and seeing words form on her side, but they weren't there on mine, which made them subjunctive: wish or feeling, less than fact. Ellipsis meant absence, nothing in the bell jar, no proof—not a specimen. The dots waved like trills on Chopin's staves, turn them how you will.

She could be typing anything. And she'd caught me, too.

The prospect should have horrified me. The texts I'd drafted in our thread were only some of the total, and all the drafts together only showed a fraction of how frequently I thought about her, and I'd composed a few a day. Edith might have caught me every time for all I knew.

But if she saw the dots, it meant she was watching.

Also, I wanted her to know.

I mouthed it and laughed, properly this time, free of the polo neck. I love Edith and I want her to know.

I rang. The dial tone beeped like dots put to music.

50

I n my last week at the flat, I rang to get the tap fixed. The landlord's agent listed spurious damages to take from the deposit. I signed. From Julian's instructions I learned the cleaning lady's name was Lea and that I was to buy her flowers. "Maybe see you again," she said, and I said: "Maybe." Packing went quickly. Most of what Julian owned had fitted in his suitcase, and I'd cleared out Edith's things some time ago.

I brought the new teacher, Sadie, around to meet the kids. Unlike Madison, she was actually from Madison. Refreshingly, she said nothing at all about Ireland. The students said we looked alike. When Sadie had left the room, Katie Cheung told me conspiratorially that I was prettier. Since haiku-gate, she'd been my favorite. Many brought cards, including the ones whose names I forgot. One way of seeing this was that their parents were deluded about my working conditions and thought I had a lot more time and mental energy to bond with their child than I did. Another was that they were kind people and I'd affected their lives more than I knew. Both things, I decided, were true at once. I couldn't quite well up at leaving a workplace that only hired white people and then wouldn't let us piss, but I was glad the kids liked me.

Julian had sent me pictures of his Frankfurt apartment. It didn't look like anyone lived there yet, but nor had the place in Mid-Levels. "It's strange without you," he'd said on the phone. Later I'd texted: are you missing the marxist invective or. He'd replied: Home is where there's a small Irish person calling for you to be guillotined.

I went to the agency to hand back the keys. "Did you have a nice stay?" the man asked.

I said I had.

Then I started the real journey. It was after morning rush hour, so the outdoor escalator was going up. Instead, I walked fifteen minutes to Sai Ying Pun station. The turnstiles beeped tautologically. I checked the map to make sure it was Island line. Cantonese throat, Mandarin, canned British voice: the train to Chai Wan is arriving. Please let passengers exit first.

My bag was light. I'd given away most of my clothes. On the phone to Mam about the move, I'd mooted throwing them down the garbage chute. She'd said that would be a waste. "I know," I'd said, "but so was buying them." Then I decided they'd lose their history faster if I donated them. Soon they'd stretch around other people and crease where their knees and elbows bent. If I'd dumped them, they'd have gone on fitting me.

Cantonese, Mandarin, British: next station, Central. I alighted, as did roughly half of Hong Kong. The suits had all looked black to me until Julian said: that's too formal for work. In fact, they were craven grays and blues. Children carried schoolbags the size of their torsos, and their nannies carried instruments the size of the children. One ahead dropped their stuffed Hello Kitty and blocked my path. I refrained from forcing my way around them. It would indicate I was in a hurry. I did seem, though, to be tapping my foot.

On the first escalator up to the concourse, I stood to the right and searched for my Octopus. If I had it ready, she wouldn't see me fumbling at the turnstile.

They ate octopus, too, in Hong Kong. It was versatile. My second month there, one of Julian's friends had described the Octopus card, an item I owned, by comparing it to the Oyster, one I didn't. Then Julian said most Londoners had switched to debit now. They'd had a long conversation about England to which I could add nothing, sparked by a public transport card I used every day and hadn't needed explained. And that was British men.

I had no single anecdote which said: and that was Edith. But my foot was tapping again.

Leaving Central station felt like going up into the clouds. Really you were just tunneling back out from underground, but I could never quite believe that. I looked up at the escalators, the longest I'd ever seen, and thought the sky was next.

One more to the concourse.

Edith had said Exit A, just beside Bank of China. I'd typed it in my notes, found it on Maps, and screenshotted it in case my data didn't work. She'd be waiting when I got there. I'd considered coming earlier—but whenever I planned to show up, she'd know, and she'd arrive just a little beforehand. That way I'd be walking and she'd be standing still.

The black brush of hair just up. And her bag.

I saw her.

Of course—up the escalator. She'd reach the top soon and march on. I'd do so, too, check my hair in my phone camera, and then go to the exit. She'd be standing there at A off Connaught Road and would look up with a surprised half smile as I approached. Our coats were both beige. It was as though we'd planned it, mainly because we had. Brushes to paint with, brushes to write with: composed.

I cut into the climbing commuters on my left. The man below me protested, not in English and not in Cantonese either. Edith stood there half a staircase up.

My calves burnt, the man ahead was fast, the one below was

gaining on me, and I climbed. I laughed at how close I was. A little faster and I'd reach her step. What would I say? I didn't know. I'd see her and see. She'd ask what I was doing and I'd say—I didn't know.

I overtook the man above, then the next one, and then there was space to run. So I did. It was somewhat ironic to sprint up an escalator that had been built to spare me that very exertion. Somewhat—but I didn't care.

ACKNOWLEDGMENTS

I would be nowhere without my agent, Harriet Moore. Thank you to Lettice Franklin and Megan Lynch, as well as the teams they work with at W&N and Ecco. I've had a lot of opportunities along the way, but I'd especially like to thank Deirdre Madden, Sally Rooney, and Ailbhe Malone.

Once you add up the stages of production, hundreds of people have helped to create and distribute this book. I'm grateful to them all. Thank you especially to the booksellers, who work harder than anyone to get books into the hands of readers.

I had a full-time teaching job when I wrote *Exciting Times*, but I earned enough money to pay rent, and I didn't have any caregiving responsibilities. It's much harder to write without those conditions in place. Everyone deserves to write books if they want to. That will never be possible in a world where billionaires exist, but it's possible in a humane one; thank you to everyone who's working and organizing to get us there.

Above all, thank you to my friends and family.